the **americas**

also in **the americas** series

Breathing, In Dust by Tim Z. Hernandez

Changó, the Biggest Badass by Manuel Zapata Olivella

The Last Reader by David Toscana

Symphony in White

Symphony in White

Adriana Lisboa

Translated from the Portuguese by Sarah Green

Edited by Irene Vilar

Texas Tech University Press

This book is typeset in Fairfield. The paper used in this book meets the minimum requirements of ANSI/NISO Z39.48-1992 (R1997). ♾

Library of Congress Cataloging-in-Publication Data
Lisboa, Adriana, 1970–
[Sinfonia em branco. English]
Symphony in white / Adriana Lisboa ; translated from the Portuguese by Sarah Green ; edited by Adriana Lisboa and Irene Vilar.
p. cm.—(The Americas series)
Summary: "Tells the story of two sisters, Clarice and Maria Inês, raised in rural Brazil in the 1960s and educated in Rio de Janeiro in the 1970s. Also presenting the perspectives of men they have loved, men they married, and the girls' parents, past events are revealed that help to explain how the two sisters' lives unfold"—Provided by publisher.
ISBN 978-0-89672-671-0 (hardcover : alk. paper)
I. Vilar, Irene. II. Title.
PQ9698.422.I73S5613 2010
869.3'42—dc22

2009053362

Printed in the United States of America
10 11 12 13 14 15 16 17 18 / 9 8 7 6 5 4 3 2 1

Texas Tech University Press | Box 41037 | Lubbock, Texas 79409-1037 USA
800.832.4042 | ttup@ttu.edu | www.ttupress.org

Si c'est inutile de pleurer, je crois qu'il faut quand même pleurer. Parce que le désespoir c'est tangible. Ça reste. Le souvenir du désespoir, ça reste. Quelquefois ça tue.

If it is useless to cry, I believe one must cry all the same. Because despair is tangible. It lingers on. The memory of despair, it lingers on. Sometimes it kills.

MARGUERITE DURAS
Écrire

Contents

Symphony in White

A Butterfly, a Forbidden Quarry

It would still be a while before she arrived.

The muggy summer afternoon floated up from the road in dust. Everything was quiet, swollen with drowsiness. A man with eyes so pale they were almost transparent pretended to watch the road, but his eyes actually searched out shards of memory like a child gathering up shells off the sand at a beach. Occasionally the present interrupted, imposed itself, and he thought, I'm going to use *dirt* in my next piece. Then the brown and arid and dusty world once more shrank to reveal a girl in white, the girl from a Whistler painting.

Tomás remembered her. But his memory was uncertain, fragmented, pieces of a prehistoric monster's skeleton, buried and preserved by chance, impossible to reconstruct in its entirety. Thirty years later. Two hundred million years later.

The dog slept at his feet and dreamed. At times it moaned. At one point it lifted its black and white head with a start and began to chew on its paw to remove a chigoe flea. The cook Jorgina's guinea fowl repeated their litany that she heard without paying any attention. It was a lusterless afternoon, like a piece of old rubber. The bougainvilleas bloomed wildly, almost aggressively.

The dog, which didn't have a name, had simply chosen that house as its own and considered itself the rightful owner of the leftovers the cook was in the habit of placing on a piece of newspaper twice a day, next to the wash tank. The dog finished its operation of removing the chigoe flea and once more dozed off.

Tomás was not a happy man. Nor was he unhappy. He considered himself *well adjusted* and for that he had paid the price that he felt was fair and had received the appropriate interest-dividends-monetary corrections. He had abdicated certain territories. He had abandoned the fantasy of an empire. He reigned only over himself and over that shack forgotten in the middle of insignificant crops and roads that turned into dust during the dry season and into mud during the rainy season. When he went to live there, he realized it was the end of his dreams. And now he thought of perhaps using dirt in his next piece. His thoughts were so small, a hint of perfume a woman might leave in the air.

Far away a plane passed over without making a sound. There were no airports nearby. It was surely headed toward the Galeão or Santos Dumont airport in the state capital of Rio de Janeiro.

The cook Jorgina, who had lost most of her teeth and now proudly sported very white dentures, silently approached Tomás and placed a steaming, rich-smelling cup of coffee on the cast iron table on the front porch. She was a woman of few words. She felt that they were as treacherous as an animal spying on its prey and were almost always unfair. She glanced at the weather and let out a meaningless sigh. She then went back inside to the stove where the rice, the beans, the pot roast bubbled.

At a distance, Tomás recognized Ilton Xavier's new pickup, which sped along the road, exhaling dust. All of these discreet movements were like the signs of a sleeping body's breathing, nothing more.

The coffee was very sweet, too sweet, but Tomás had learned to like it that way. It was the way of the people from those parts, light on the coffee, heavy on the sugar. The dog, which was being pestered by a horsefly, lifted its head and in one swift movement caught the insect in mid-flight with its mouth.

Tomás regarded his bare legs without interest. On his skin, like tattoos, were the rough signs of that place, so far from concrete and asphalt: innumerable mosquito, tick, horsefly, and other insect bites, a small scar on his left calf, where the larva of a botfly had been removed at the health center in Jabuticabais. At his feet a laborious trail of ants carved a living groove on the ground.

In the small sitting room with a worn-out red cement floor, his paintings were piled waiting for Cândido to pick them up on the weekend, paintings unpretentious in size and purpose at a hundred reais each, destined to decorate middle-class country living rooms, physicians' waiting rooms, modest law offices. The notary public in Jabuticabais had bought two, according to Cândido. One he hung in his office, the other was a wedding present for a niece. Occasionally someone would request a portrait at double the price, which made Cândido happy, but Tomás's mood didn't seem to change much. It remained as uniform as the dry afternoon.

In the landscape paintings there was almost always a road that led to nowhere. That disappeared behind a tree, or around a curve, or down a slope. And in the lower right-hand corner was the signature of someone who signed his paintings only because the buyers demanded he do so. Earlier, when he was twenty years old, Tomás refused to pollute any of his paintings with a signature that ruined the overall composition, like someone coughing in the middle of a concert or lights coming on in a movie theater before the film was over.

Now, he did whatever his clients wanted, and for those clients his signature lent authenticity to the painting, even if it was the signature of an unknown artist. He signed his name with black paint and the handwriting of a child.

Tomás lit a cigarette and a spiral of smoke rose up like a charmed snake. For an instant it gave the impression of sculpting a female figure, but that soon dissipated into the air. Tired from sleeping, the dog sat up, scratched its ear with its hind paw, and left the paw in mid-air for an instant. It looked into the distance and perceived something that escaped the man. It turned back its head and saw the open door behind and had a canine premonition. Then it went two yards forward to lie down, where the grass was higher and perhaps cooler.

There was nothing really new for Tomás anymore. Words were sparse, a consequence of spending most of his time with a cook who didn't like to talk and communicated by smiles and monosyllables. Except when he periodically went to Jabuticabais, the nearest town, and did his meager shopping. Other than that, there were the visits from his friend Clarice and the visits to his friend Clarice, which only went to show there was nothing really new anymore.

His race was run and Tomás could now sit in the shade, in front of the finish line, which happened to coincide with the starting line, as if he hadn't moved at all or as if he had made a huge circle, 360 degrees. So the only thing left was for him to observe the earth's rotation and the almost imperceptible change of seasons. Within this reality, Clarice's company fit in without demands, without raising a ruckus, without causing any disturbances that might require answers, as silent as everything else. If a spiral of smoke sculpted a female figure, that figure would not be Clarice. However, as Tomás had to recognize, it might still evoke that other woman, in spite of everything. The woman he would see again the next day. A woman his memory always dressed in white.

Many years before, that woman was still simply Maria Inês. And she had just planted a money tree in the company of her second cousin who was still simply João Miguel.

It's still not growing, complained João Miguel.

Maria Inês shrugged her shoulders and said you just aren't patient. You think it's as simple as that? That we plant a seed and it starts to grow at that very instant? You have to wait a long time.

How long?

It depends. Days, weeks.

That long?

She didn't answer. She smoothed the dirt down with motherly tenderness, then turned her eyes to follow a butterfly that flew across the small space to the quarry, where it leaped daringly into the abyss.

Now pay attention, don't you go telling my father that we were here. It's forbidden, said Maria Inês.

Forbidden?

Yes. We're not allowed to come here. It's really dangerous.

That made João Miguel afraid, but at the same time it was obvious that a money tree, like the one he and his second cousin had just planted, should be in a secret place.

It had taken the two children an hour to hike up the hill, crossing the pasture and the small woods at the top (like a remaining patch of hair on an almost completely bald head), infesting themselves with ticks, up to the edge of the quarry where families of lizards lay camouflaged in the sun.

Up there, leaning over the highest rock, they could see the

whole world, or at least what, to Maria Inês, nine years old, seemed to be the whole world. To one side, the river, a thin string of gold, the animals in the pasture like miniatures, the house and corral, colorful plastic toys. To the other side, the emptiness accentuated by the abrupt precipice. Below, in the abandoned headquarters of the Ipês Farm, ghosts wandered about, round snails leisurely scuffed the walls, and plants grew on the roof. The paint on the windows peeled off little by little. Day by day everything aged and became more secretive. More painful.

Did I ever tell you about the Ipês Farm? she asked João Miguel.

He lied, saying no only because he wanted to hear the story again.

She began: they say the owner went crazy because he caught his wife with another man. He went to the kitchen, got a big knife. They say he was drunk. Maybe he was crazy. He got the knife and he killed his wife! Can you imagine that? With seventeen stabs. The other guy managed to escape and call the police.

Maria Inês paused, appraised the silence on the tip of her tongue, and felt its sweet and sour taste, like tamarind candy.

She then continued, competent storyteller, relating how pacific Jabuticabais's scanty population became enraged, how they rose up like a tidal wave, invaded the police station, and lynched the assassin right in the middle of the street, with sticks and stones and then fire. His daughter, the embittered child who inherited those lands, was forced to mature early, like fruit in a greenhouse. Her name was Lindaflor. Some said she was as blond as an angel, others swore she had flaming red hair and very white skin, or that she was as dark as a native Brazilian, with thick, straight hair. One moment she was sneaky like her mother, another violent like her father, another she was sweet and insane. The information as to her whereabouts also varied. She was with her aunt and uncle in the nearby town of Friburgo. With her cousins in Rio de Janeiro. She had moved abroad. Maria Inês couldn't clarify any of that with her parents, because, of course, that topic was also forbidden.

All things forbidden seduced her in the same proportion that they repressed Clarice, her older sister, who was about to turn thirteen and was as obedient as a trained dog, who never went near the quarry and never asked questions about the Ipês Farm tragedy.

Do you want to know what I'm going to do with my share of the money, the day when it's all grown and full of fruit-coins? Maria Inês asked her second cousin, referring to the tree. I'm going to travel, she said. By ship, to Europe.

João Miguel said my father travels a lot. Even to Europe, by ship and by plane.

There was an apparent detachment in his remark.

Planting a money tree using a coin for a seed had been her idea, naturally—the inventive Maria Inês, the daring, the curious. She looked at her cousin with compassion. Whenever João Miguel remembered his father and turned as somber as a rainy Monday, she was filled with the desire to protect him, her poor abandoned cousin.

He traveled a lot, his father. All the way to Europe, all the way to his native Italy. By plane. With his lover. While his wife wasted away in a clinic for the mentally ill. Of course knowing those details was forbidden, but Maria Inês had her ways of overhearing the adults' conversations.

With his lover. And his only son left forgotten behind for the three-month summer vacation on his cousins' farm, in the backlands of the state.

Poor João Miguel, said Maria Inês, and her words were one-third sincerity, one-third irony, and one-third indifference. Her fingers softly grazed her second cousin and husband's wrist, which he had injured in a tennis match that Sunday morning, thirty-five years after that morning they had climbed a hill and gone close to a forbidden quarry to plant a money tree.

After her caress, as gentle as the brush of an insect's wing, Maria Inês put her reading glasses back on and listlessly dug her face into the newspaper.

She said the Sunday editions were stupid and never had anything important to say.

And João Miguel said that was exactly the idea. Sunday editions for Sunday readers.

Maria Inês continued to turn the pages, pausing here and there. She leafed through the thin magazine filled with gossip about American actors, fashion, and beauty tips. An interview. A health insurance ad. A shallow, lackadaisical column. She only stopped again to drink her last sip of coffee, strong and black, like in Italy, where she had learned to drink her coffee that way. She placed the white cup back onto the white saucer that sat on the table with a crystal top and a white marble base.

It was boiling hot and the color of the morning was an unreliable blue. Too intense, an artificial oil-painting blue, mixed on an artist's palette.

On the streets of Rio de Janeiro, unselfconscious, overweight women paraded cellulite-covered thighs bursting from their short shorts and loose, cropped shirts that revealed chubby arms and chubby stomachs beneath fleshy breasts. Refined ladies with thin eyebrows walked on the sidewalks with brassiere straps peeking out from under their blouses. On their foreheads, temples, and above their lips smeared with red lipstick, sweat resisted their linen handkerchiefs. Men took off their shirts, exposing toasted, sedentary bellies. Almost everyone was too tan, faces red, swimsuit strap marks, thin and white, decorating backs, skin peeling off, lips swollen.

The heat was everywhere and it did little good to seek out the deceitful comfort of the sea, because the sun was baking hot even as the cold salt water tried to convince everyone there was some relief. On the contrary, the water made the sunburns more severe. The heat was in the sand, on the sidewalks, in the window shops, on the asphalt, in the trees, everywhere, in the air, on the walls, in the open-mouthed, tongue-dripping dogs, on the papayas on top of the table, stamped like an extra hue in the treacherous blue of the sky.

In Maria Inês and João Miguel Azzopardi's large living room, there was, however, an anesthetic known as a twenty-three-thousand-BTU air conditioner. The apartment in the Upper Leblon neighborhood was an aquarium and in its refrigerated waters floated a few secret fish, most of them nameless.

Everything was white. White sofa, white walls. White ideas. A large quantity of white marble. Some brushed aluminum, as in the two chairs. Some satinwood, as in the shelves.

The money used to purchase all of that had not sprouted from the tree they had once planted but from the natural handing down of the business from the *vecchio* Azzopardi, Azzopardi senior, to Azzopardi junior, João Miguel.

That year, like every year, the *vecchio* would receive his guests in his native Tuscany villa, where he had gone to live after his retirement, on turning seventy. Full of vitality and a desire to drink Chianti and to have ever younger girlfriends.

João Miguel's flight would leave at night. Eduarda had decided to go with her mother to see her Aunt Clarice, in the backlands of the state, a place where tourists never set foot.

According to protocol, Maria Inês would have accompanied João Miguel. With her long body, any imperfections softened by well-chosen clothing, her face that had learned to smile properly, her perfumed presence, never overbearing, never overly unassuming, not unlike a new language learned to such perfection that it almost extinguished the memory of the original language.

Still hidden inside, however, was the rough language of an *improper* girl, who had chosen the farm instead of *Papa* Azzopardi's villa. Her own life, instead of his. Her own secrets, as well. Her own voluntary exile.

She folded the newspaper over four times, removed her reading glasses, and told João Miguel to be sure to use ice compresses and take anti-inflammatory pills.

João Miguel made a vague gesture with his hand. He didn't consider Maria Inês's medical opinions entirely trustworthy, in spite of her diploma. She knew this and shrugged her shoulders and said if it starts hurting, call Vargas. He's the specialist. His number's in my address book.

She stood and crossed the room.

I'm going to take a bath, she said, leaving a hint of perfume behind in the air as her bare feet touched the cold floor.

The bathroom was not air-conditioned and it was hard to avoid sweating in there. Maria Inês saw the miniature ornamental garden that grew on the far side of the shower stall. A miniature garden inside the bathroom with small swollen-leafed plants and delicate flowers. If Eduarda were still a child, she could play with her dolls there.

Maria Inês began to undress in front of the mirror. With a quick gesture she took off her nightgown and once more faced that intimate, everyday truth, her body. Her hips were a bit too wide and her stomach was far from being as flat as a board. Her breasts, which had nursed a child, still looked like adolescent breasts, small and fragile. She had a scar from an acute appendicitis five years earlier. Removing her panties, the remains of her C-section, a small, curved scar about four inches long, was still visible.

Her dark eyes drew closer to her reflection and she plucked a few superfluous hairs from the once thick eyebrows, now so well-shaped. She thought of João Miguel and his injured wrist, then tried to forget about them both. It wasn't a good idea to have second thoughts about decisions made so long ago. João Miguel and Maria Inês both seemed to be at peace. The years built up sediments and smoothed out any foolhardiness. Maria Inês no longer felt pain when her tweezers took hold of a hair and pulled it out from the root, her skin had gotten used to it.

She dipped her feet into the bathtub, first the right one, and then the left. The tide rose until it reached her neck, and the water had a pleasant neutral spirit. It was cool, which was also good, since in that bathroom, in that city, in that season, it was hard to avoid sweating.

The nape of her neck rested on the edge of the tub. Maria Inês closed her eyes and took a deep breath and for a brief moment thought that it just might be possible.

Clarice observed without interest the new pickup that Ilton Xavier (*her* Ilton Xavier) had bought a few weeks earlier and that now rolled down the dirt road leaving in its wake a cloud of dust like an afterthought. Ilton Xavier had ceased to be *hers* long ago, but some old habits remained, like that possessive adjective she thoughtlessly used, *my* Ilton Xavier. It was not a major fault.

She was leaning out the living room window watching life go by on a still afternoon—the knowledge, which she had acquired upon turning her present age of forty-eight—*time stands still, but creatures pass by*. She wrote it down in a notebook, like a confession, not letting it bother her that writing thoughts in notebooks was, or at least had been, her sister's habit. It didn't matter. After so many years and the whole story, everything was quite relative. Even confessions jotted down in a notebook were, after all, silly.

Forty-eight. And lumpy scars on her naked wrists. Clarice allowed her eyes to scan the land (there wasn't that much) that had belonged to her father, Afonso Olímpio, and which she had sold without regret, keeping only the isolated area with the buildings, where she lived. She saw the old farmhand's house where Tomás, her sister's old lover, now lived and worked on his paintings, devoid of ambition—landscapes stripped of any verve. Still still lifes. Abstracts that didn't mean anything and had no desire to mean anything. Listless portraits. Tomás seemed to pursue mediocrity with the same perseverance with which, decades earlier, he had pursued a supposedly *superior talent* destined for recognition by humanity. He had turned all of that inside out to survive the loss of a woman. And the absence of whatever it was that she had extracted from him and taken away.

Clarice also saw fences covered with the hanging *erva-de-passarinho* weeds, and other fences, a bit farther, white wood, recently painted. She saw the cattle standing motionless in the pasture. Most of them huddled up under the shade of a mango tree, slowly moving their jaws and flicking insects off with their tails. Then she turned her back to the window and saw the photograph of Otacília, her mother.

With her thumbs, Clarice once more felt the twin scars left by the Olfa knife on each wrist. She usually hid them by wearing a watch and bracelets on those rare occasions that she was in public.

She didn't need any of that at the moment, she was also barefoot, wearing an old, over-sized white t-shirt smeared with clay, and her thick hair was pulled back into a bun. It was the unpretentious Clarice. There was no wedding band on her left ring finger. The one that before (long before) had the name *Ilton Xavier* engraved on the inside had been sold some years back.

The furniture in that house had survived the onslaught of time. The mustard-colored upholstery of the large recliner was threadbare in several spots, as was Clarice's memory as it wandered along the days in which one could lean back there after lunch, in the middle of a hot, dry afternoon, and doze off without a worry in the world. In front of the fireplace there were still some logs where spiders wove their webs. The poker was completely rusted. The rug was faded, but clean. And Otacília's photograph was only slightly yellowed. It remained hanging on the same nail and it wasn't Clarice's place to remove it, it wasn't her place to take a position in relation to her mother's memory, she had no right, because Otacília had been almost a stranger to her.

On top of the coffee table, next to the old ashtray, was a book. Thomas Mann's *Death in Venice*. A book that would have been radically forbidden by Otacília and Afonso Olímpio, now desecrating what might still remain of their will.

As if to correct this lapse, the oratory, its wooden doors open, still sheltered the image of the Virgin Mary with Christ on her lap. In a soapstone vase (bought in Ouro Preto, in Afonso Olímpio's native state of Minas Gerais), there were dried flowers that let off the odor of plain everyday things.

Three of the four rooms were dormant. Once a week the windows were opened and the sunlight would gently caress the floor. The three rooms were swept and dusted, the furniture was polished, the lizards and spiders hid in the cracks waiting for the activity to cease.

The other room was the one Clarice occupied, the same room she had occupied an eternity ago and from which she had never managed to escape. Why not recognize it? Now that her parents were nothing more than a pair of matching names on a tombstone in the small Jabuticabais cemetery, and most of the land had been sold, and the warm breath of disuse had entered every crack of the premises—the empty corral, the empty barn, the storehouses, the garage for the tractor, the useless motor from the tractor and its rusted body—Clarice could now recognize that she had never taken a single step. Overcoming her fears didn't mean movement. It was more like a blank page where no word cared to be written.

With a long sigh, she let the afternoon go and watched the evening's first bats as they took flight and softly whistled through the trees.

She would pretend to read *Death in Venice* as the static electricity burned the air, a prelude to rain. In the huge quarry that sat atop the nearest hill, a laggard butterfly opened its multicolored wings and launched itself into the abyss.

Death in Venice would have been a forbidden book. But now Clarice could accompany Gustav von Aschenbach leaving his residence on Prinzregentenstrasse, Munich, for a walk, at the beginning of May in an indeterminate year (19 . . . , right on the first line). She no longer had to please Otacília to win her love.

As a child, she even wished she could read minds in order to anticipate Otacília's every wish and desire. But nothing seemed to please her, neither Clarice's diligence and obedience, nor Maria Inês's insubordinate vivacity, nor the appropriate solicitousness of Afonso Olímpio, with his beautiful crystal-clear Minas Gerais accent and the aroma of his pipe that he smoked in silence, in the late afternoon. A few years had been enough to obscure Otacília, to cloud her aquamarine blue eyes, to turn her into a cold, sleepless night.

Clarice closed the book she pretended to read, she didn't bother to mark her place because she would have to start it all over again, once more Gustav von Aschenbach on Prinzregentenstrasse (in 19 . . .). She raised her eyes to the photograph of Otacília in her wedding dress and spied a small silverfish dragging itself across the photograph, limp, absent.

There were no reproductions of Whistler's painting in the few books that Tomás still owned. *The White Girl*—or: *Symphony in White, No. 1*. With so much wandering on the edges of life it was only natural that material possessions were left behind here and there, like flakes of dead skin. Tomás had sold what little remained to purchase that scrap of land where a morose shack apologized for its existence, where guinea fowl repeated their litany, where the cook Jorgina made coffee that was too weak and too sweet, where a dog with no name and no owner dreamed and always devoured its meals as if it were starving to death and then lay there with its stomach swollen. Almost all of the books had disappeared, together with the greater part of his ambitions.

He waited. Like Clarice, who was his neighbor and whose nearby house he could distinguish in the twilight, among the old eucalyptus and pine trees.

The dog seemed to have ended its day and dragged itself across the floor to continue sleeping on the living room rug. A multitude of stars began to appear in the January sky. Out there it was possible to see them in the Milky Way's porous band, floating in a night so different from city nights, where stars faded and were outshone by other lights. Perhaps it wasn't going to rain after all, even though the afternoon had ended heavy with expectation.

Tomás could hear and smell something frying in the kitchen. At his feet a half-dead moth had ceased its useless struggle while a funeral procession of hungry black ants dragged it across the floor.

At his distant twenty years of age, everything was so different. And, nevertheless, it might be correct to say all the later events were already there.

One day, the police invaded the small apartment in the Flamengo neighborhood, which his parents had bought only two months earlier. Looking for *subversive* books. There weren't any left; they had been ripped apart and flushed down the toilet. One terrifying night, Tomás watched the plane take off carrying his parents into exile. One morning, Tomás woke up and realized that he was twenty years old and all alone. Alone, in every sense. He had at least twenty options before him, which is why he smiled when he caught sight of the young girl on the balcony of an apartment in the nearby building. She was dressed in white and her hair was loose. Long hair, thick and dark, wavy. It couldn't have been otherwise: she was the Whistler girl.

Tomás had ambitious sketchbooks scattered about the Flamengo apartment. His canvases kept growing in size. The air was filled with the smell of oil and acrylic paints.

Pencils, blending stumps, charcoal, pastel chalks, jars of gouache paint and India ink, brushes were spread out on top of the dining room table. Previously, that was the place where not only had they eaten their meals, but also had conducted inflamed clandestine Communist Party discussions. His father was a journalist. His mother, a law student and president of the academic board at the Catholic University. They had code names taken from the Old Testament—she was Esther, he was Solomon.

In Tomás's dreams, there was a series of museums he had never visited, and sophisticated art galleries, and biennials, expositions, panoramas, retrospectives, where his curiosity loved to roam. However, his talent, confused, wrestled with itself, barely productive or overly productive, disorganized and capricious. As if all the possibilities were to introduce themselves at the same time and as if the present moment were the very last. At the same time, as if nothing was so urgent it could upstage his Sunday morning sleep or the lethargy of the sun warming his skin.

Without borders, order, or continents, Tomás's talent spread out and often lost its way, or instead flitted about the nooks of the apartment like an insect lost in the dark. Moments of discipline were reduced to the few private lessons he gave, an alternative to looking for a job (which, anyway, he was in danger of not finding, being a *persona non grata*, because of his parents).

He discovered the girl in the apartment building next door almost by chance. It only took one glance to immediately think of that painter who had often combined color and music in the titles of his paintings. He knew some of them from books. *Nocturne in*

Black and Gold, Nocturne in Blue and Green, Harmony in Violet and Yellow. Symphony in White. Seeing her, that girl, Tomás immediately thought of doing a painting after Whistler, inspired by his *Symphony in White*. He was fated to fall madly in love.

The following decades revealed to him all his regrettable mistakes. He no longer had a book with a reproduction of that painting. Where he could see it and rekindle that same miserable feeling of powerlessness. He had said too few words, taken too few positions. But maybe all of that, like Whistler, like the glorious futures, was actually forgotten.

Now, however, Tomás remembered, even though his memory was frayed and he could see through it as if it were a piece of worn-out cloth. And there was no way not to remember. At the age of twenty, he would get drunk on rum and Coca-Cola and would sleep for ten or twelve hours straight. Today he had to content himself with insomnia.

For different reasons, Clarice also waited. It was past nine o'clock when she put on a pair of jeans under her big t-shirt, slipped on her flip-flops, and penetrated the almost total darkness of the path that led to Tomás's door.

Many years earlier, the house where he now lived had been part of Afonso Olímpio and Otacília's property: a farmhand's cottage, rustic, too insignificant to deserve aesthetic considerations, with a blank wall and a porch with the same red cement flooring of the tiny living room, the bedroom, and the kitchen. The kitchen, spacious compared to the rest, had previously been the room where meals were eaten, visitors were received, and, close to the wood-burning stove, the chill of winter nights was shooed away. Before, there had been no electricity, but instead candles and oil lamps where insects burned to death. Today bare lamp bulbs hung from the ceiling, revealing wires, stripped of chandeliers or light fixtures.

Are you busy? Clarice asked, pushing open the door that was always half-open.

She had no affectations with Tomás. Her wrists with the scars like thin, serious lips were visible, without shame. A few curly strands of hair fell over her ears, escaping from her loose bun. She wasn't wearing earrings. She was not, never had been, fair-skinned like Maria Inês, even if she went months without exposing herself to the sun.

You're not painting? she repeated the question, even after Tomás shook his head.

Not today, he said, and she understood.

Somewhat shyly, she asked you wouldn't have anything to drink, would you? A beer, or even a liqueur?

I thought you'd stopped, he said, although there was no censorship in his voice.

I did, it's true. But today, you know.

Tomás nodded his head in agreement, but answered no, it's been a while since I went shopping in town, and I finished off my last bottle of vodka yesterday.

Clarice nudged the corner of the rug with her foot and said that's too bad.

I can give you some coffee or we can pick some oranges and make juice.

Orange juice with vodka would have been great, Clarice said, smiling. A screwdriver. Reminds me of parties from way back when.

A light bulb made a weak effort to illuminate the front porch. Everything outside the house was pitch black, but Tomás and

Clarice were used to the dark. The dog followed them to the door. But it didn't go any farther. It didn't circle the rabbit cages and the simple thatched-roof chicken coop or hop down the few dirt steps to reach the small orchard where a few orange trees, a lime tree, an *acerola* tree, a papaya tree, and the always present guava trees grew. Submerged in the night, the trees seemed to be half-asleep spirits, swaying in the light breeze, or possibly of their own will. Fireflies twinkled in the tree branches, and far beyond, the countless stars.

Clarice and Tomás picked six ripe oranges. When she was still a girl, long before Rio de Janeiro, before Ilton Xavier, when that farmhand's cottage had not even dreamed of Tomás, Clarice and her sister would climb the guava trees and stuff themselves on the ripe fruit where worms frequently feasted.

Have you ever thought about how many worms we must have eaten without realizing it? Maria Inês suggested one day.

Clarice made a face of disgust and vehemently denied that possibility: we always pay lots of attention.

You can never pay enough attention. Maybe we've already swallowed pieces of guava worms. Just a head, or a tail. And if we swallowed a head? Do guava worms have brains? We ate guava worm brains, Clarice.

Maria Inês took a morbid pleasure in anything that could annoy, shock, frighten, or repulse. When their cousin João Miguel arrived for his summer vacations, she always greeted him with a toad or a beetle in her hands, but that seemed to be an expression of her love for him, for it was also true that she took care of their cousin and, although she was younger, protected him from everything and everybody with her almost arrogant courage.

Clarice didn't know anything about Whistler's painting. She wasn't even aware of its existence. She pretended to taste vodka as she sipped her orange juice. She was sitting on Tomás's living room floor, her back against the sofa that Cândido had discarded a few years earlier because it was already too old.

Reminded of Cândido, Clarice asked how's that guy who buys your paintings, the gallery owner?

He's still interested in your work, Tomás answered, tilting his head toward a marble female torso Clarice had sculpted, which occupied a shelf suspended on the wall. The trunk curved over to the side, leaning slightly back, and the shoulders were open. There were no legs, no arms, no head. On her uneven skin, intentionally rough, the chisel marks were still apparent. As if that small piece was meant to be incomplete. Half sculpture, half misshapen stone. Perhaps it was a self-portrait that, bordering on the invisible, remembered something dangerous.

Clarice looked at her bare feet: uncared for, small. With detachment, she studied the sculpture she had given to Tomás.

Truth be said, they were not thinking about their art at all. The main topic was her, Maria Inês. Always her. Now she was coming, she was arriving the next day. Maria Inês was always at a distance of one or at the most two simple associations, but her name was never mentioned. She weighed down on them much heavier as an absence.

Trio for Horn, Violin, and Piano

In the early hours of the morning that Maria Inês was yanked into life, the God of her parents wept calmly onto the land. Perhaps that was why, ever since she was a child, she always enjoyed a gentle rain, as if those teardrops were etched in her memory the same way the dark color of her eyes and hair were ingrained in her genetic code.

She was named after her paternal great-aunt who had died crazy, but her parents, Otacília and Afonso Olímpio, did not believe that this was a bad omen. In Afonso Olímpio's family they had the habit of repeating names. His name, for example: Afonso was because of his father. Olímpio was because of his uncle. His brother, who still lived in Minas Gerais, was Mariano Olímpio, because of another uncle, whose own name had come from an ancestor named Mariana who had been recorded as being half saint. If it's possible that someone can be a saint halfway.

Maria Inês's head was as long as a cigar, but it didn't worry her mother. Clarice had also been born with a minor defect or two that her first months of life had corrected.

Otacília and Afonso Olímpio were not so young any longer, they had already passed the age considered appropriate to have children in those days, but they had married late.

Otacília was twenty-eight and by that age her mother had already given birth to five children. Her brother-in-law took the photograph that the priest blessed: Otacília, veil, garland, satin and lace, immortalized on the happiest and most unreal day of her life. Otacília wanted to hang her picture in a prominent spot in the living room of the house her husband had built, the main house of a small farm that was not far from her childhood home, in the vicinity of that veritable end-of-the-world called Jabuticabais. A town that wasn't even on the map. The photograph was hung close to the fireplace.

Each one of Otacília's features was, in itself, beautiful. Nature had chosen a pair of eyes the color of blue aquamarines and luscious lips, and silky black hair, and a thin waistline and firm hands, and mixed them all together, but the result was unsatisfactory. Her sisters were jealous of her blue eyes, always, but they forgave her, since they, put all together, resulted in two unquestionably beautiful girls.

Afonso Olímpio, on the other hand, inspired suspicion:

Have you noticed that he's a bit . . .

Don't you think that he's somewhat . . .

I'm not sure, I might be wrong, but to me he seems to be . . .

Kind of *mulatto*.

That *bad* hair.

Otacília interrupted, saying Afonso Olímpio is *white*, his skin is just a little darker due to the sun.

The small church in Jabuticabais heard her and Afonso Olímpio's vows on a morning freshly washed by the rain. The nearby farm breathed meekly, waiting for them, completely innocent.

Of course her marriage was never all that Otacília had imagined. But that subject was way beyond forbidden, one she could not discuss even with her sisters, the two not-aquamarine-blue-eyed beauties. She imagined that at night, under the sheets, after saying their rosary and letting down their hair, her sisters enjoyed having relations with their husbands. She wondered to herself if her mother. If the maids. If her cousins. If other women. If prostitutes (extremely forbidden). And from all her filtered pondering there was nothing left for her but a bitter stab of hopelessness, for in the end, conjecture after conjecture, she was faced with the question: *would it be different with other men?*

She had been married seven years and had two small children when she looked at her face in the mirror: She had two daughters, wrinkles that had been gathering in secret throughout those long years in a slow conspiracy, and a husband who did not match her dreams. Making love was as mechanical as peeling potatoes or darning a pair of socks. Never, in seven years, had Afonso Olímpio provided her with romance. Or an orgasm.

Her two girls were destined to grow up and make love. This magnified them to an almost unsupportable level.

Maria Inês opened her eyes and reached for the towel. Her marriage was never all that she had imagined, but that was her fault for ever having imagined, without asking herself if she would fit into the fantasy.

In the same way that a drawer in her closet was home to old notes, letters, newspaper clippings (Bernardo Águas interviews), small, obsolete fetishes, so did a part of her heart hold the remnants from her life. One day, a family, a young girl named Maria Inês. One day her childhood and a money tree. One day the boy João Miguel, the young man João Miguel, the second cousin and accomplice. One day love and lovers. And some sketches and a Whistler painting. None of that had truly existed. Everything had dissolved like an ice cube floating in the harsh heat of the summers in that city. Not Jabuticabais but the other city, the big city.

The truth was made of small, loving stabs of pain. Like sitting in the Café Florian, in Venice, she and her husband João Miguel, who spoke Italian so well. He was a polyglot, unlike Maria Inês, who barely got by with her broken English. Maria Inês got up to buy some postcards nearby, she didn't take more than ten minutes. The Florian, on the Piazza San Marco, the Florian of Proust and Wagner. And Casanova. For ten minutes João Miguel sat without Maria Inês at the table. Later, alone in her room at the hotel, she understood that vices and virtues were almost always a mere difference of perspective, and that it was not unusual for them to change places as in a Maypole dance.

She towel-dried her short hair. To think about the Florian was not a good idea. She and her husband got along well. The balance was regulated with smiles, without sex, with politeness and quick kisses, with air conditioners, without pets, with the same shared bed, with pajamas and nightgowns that no longer came off.

It was definitely not a good idea to think about the Café Florian. But the young Venetian named Paolo found his way into Maria Inês's thoughts like a sudden headache. She was crossing the Piazza San Marco through a multitude of pigeons, carrying a pile of postcards in her hands. At the table of the Florian, João Miguel had been joined by the young Venetian. In Maria Inês's hands a photograph, framed in white with *Venezia* written across the top, showed a canal with dark green water and a building with Moorish windows and a tree with bare branches leaning over a crumbling wall. *Venezia*, it said. A sharp stab of pain—nothing more.

Maria Inês remembered: the next day she had sent the postcard with the Moorish windows and the bare-branched tree to Clarice, dutifully composed with cordial words. As usual, the truth was not spoken, not even insinuated. The truth about pain and a handsome young Venetian named Paolo.

She had decided on the trip to the farm ten days earlier. On Christmas Eve. A daring decision, breaking a handful of items in the set of rules she herself had devised and adopted. She would not go with João Miguel to the domains of the *vecchio* Azzopardi, *papa* Guilio. And this was joyful and sad, like Carnival and Ash Wednesday. It was the same as realizing that the costumes were getting too tight, or were too loose, or were old, wrinkled, threadbare.

João Miguel's response to her audacity had been the most complete indifference. Maria Inês could hear him on the telephone the evening of December twenty-fourth, and he said I think for the time being we can maintain the Thursday lesson. Then his voice dropped to a murmur. It was the tennis instructor.

A fleeting chill ran down Maria Inês's arms. A handsome young Venetian at the Florian.

On Christmas Eve, her daughter Eduarda was sitting on the white sofa and put on some music that Maria Inês didn't know. The lyrics went: *There's a little black spot on the sun today*. Eduarda hummed along. She had just turned nineteen. On that Christmas Eve she heard, while João Miguel was on the phone, her mother's decision: as soon as New Year's is over, I'm going to the farm.

Immediately, Eduarda announced I'm going, too, and it was impossible for her to kid herself that she didn't see a faint trace of alarm cloud her mother's face for an instant.

At the farm, there was a forbidden quarry, an old house, a certain Ipês Farm where a man insane with jealousy had committed a crime. There was a money tree that had never sprouted.

There was more: a nine-year-old child. A half-open door. A pale breast, which was inadvertently glimpsed out of the corner of an eye. A masculine hand on a breast, vaguely pale.

The farm had once been the center of Maria Inês's life and dreams. Afterwards, it had given her nightmares. It had been ten years since she had set foot there. It had been ten years since she had seen Clarice.

Does anyone care for some wine?

João Miguel was handsome, well-dressed. With his thick, salt-and-pepper hair and his dark eyes that earlier, so much earlier, had sparkled with expectation as they planted a money tree.

His wife asked if the tennis instructor wouldn't like to come for dinner on Christmas Eve. He answered that the tennis instructor would naturally be with his own family. And Maria Inês accepted the glass of wine her husband offered her.

The family that would come for Christmas dinner was composed of some cousins and half a dozen aunts and uncles. Written on the gifts under the huge Christmas tree were the names of each person.

She examined her fingernails, manicured in the latest shade, then smoothed her dress that made her look like a piece of furniture, matching the rest of the house.

Eduarda watched her repeat those gestures that were like a rosary in the hands of an atheist. She stood up and changed the music to one of Maria Inês's CDs. Brahms, *Trio for Horn, Violin and Piano. Opus forty*. And looked at her mother again, who suddenly looked as if she might shatter.

What had made her decide to go with her mother on the trip to the farm? She didn't know. Perhaps she just wanted to be present. Like a present.

Then her aunts and uncles and cousins began to arrive with their kindly or bored smiles. The women were overdressed and had on too much make-up. One could feel the room temperature rise just by looking at them, in spite of the twenty-three thousand BTUs.

Some of the women had faces stretched by plastic surgery. And at least one of them had stuffed a pair of silicone breasts into her body. There was a slightly sad girl who sat in a corner. There was a hysterical woman (her voice sounds like the nanny's voice from the TV series, thought Eduarda) who was continually pinching and nuzzling a little girl in her lap, when she wasn't repeatedly throwing the child up in the air, making her dizzy with fear. There was an obnoxious man bragging about modern safaris to Africa. There was a slightly boring intellectual who nonetheless managed to catch Eduarda's attention with a clever joke. There was a hip young woman with a nose ring and her head practically shaved bald. With clothes bought in a second-hand store and fluorescent sneakers. There was a beardless rocker, with long hair and a Guns N' Roses t-shirt covering a sunken chest and thin arms, who studied guitar and dreamed of playing the solo in *Stairway to Heaven*.

They sipped expensive drinks and spoke of dried-up matters. They were like fish that had been caught here and there, at random, and packed into the same aquarium.

Maria Inês drank one, two, three, seven, eight glasses of wine. It killed the ants scurrying through her brain.

Her Christmas was so blue (*gelée exfoliante*) and white and silver. She and her husband exchanged innocuous smiles. After the wine began to pour lead into her thoughts, Maria Inês staggered through the living room in an awkward solo waltz and landed in the big armchair in the study. There, in the half-light, a cousin (or was it an uncle? Now what was his name?) examined the spines of the books on the shelves as his glass exhaled bubbles.

Another dissident, he said upon seeing Maria Inês.

She smiled and said I've had too much to drink.

The cousin (uncle?) sighed and said that's what I should do. I don't mean to offend you. I think you're a very cool person, but these end-of-the-year parties. . . .

Maria Inês felt like reminding him that no one was obliged to come. But solidarity made her shake her head and finish his sentence. They suck.

He turned back to look at the books. Then he said, full of self-pity, you know that Luciana and I separated.

Maria Inês had to make a huge effort to remember: Luciana, a pretty redhead. Last Christmas.

I didn't know. When?

Tomorrow it'll be a month. The girls are with her.

The fair-skinned faces of redheaded twins, still quite young, with dog-ears and matching barrettes vaguely came to mind. Mickey Mouse barrettes. She now remembered that João Miguel had said something about it, but she hadn't paid attention.

The uncle (cousin?) sat down at Maria Inês's feet.

There's something I need to tell you. He then sighed: I'm not sure you're ready to hear this.

She looked at him with a sleepy face and an expression that seemed to confirm the obvious, *I have no idea what you have to say, so I can't possibly know if I'm ready to hear it or not*. And she continued to toss the paradox around in her head: if I knew what you have to say, then perhaps I would recognize that I'm not ready to hear it, but then it would make no difference, for I would have already heard it. She laughed, but stopped immediately, because he was very serious.

I think that Luciana and your husband are having an affair. It just occurred to me. It seems that they've been getting together.

Maria Inês took a sip from her glass, a cool, white sip, and looked at the white marble floor half-covered by a rug with a geometrical design on which someone had dropped a lit cigarette, where there was now the blemish of a black circle.

It's possible. I don't know anything about it, but it's possible, she said, and then asked him if he was still involved in the film industry and if he thought *Four Days in September* had a chance of winning the Oscar.

They came to tell Maria Inês that a relative from Manaus was on the telephone. She excused herself from the cousin and went to answer in her bedroom. Merry Christmas to you, too.

Then she threw herself onto the bed. She was tired for no real reason. Tired with no right to be tired and for that reason all the more tired.

Eduarda came to the door to see her mother, big-little, and remembered the word game she would recite, as a child: a tall-short fat-skinny man sitting down-standing up on a stone-wooden bench wordlessly said that a deaf man heard a mute say that a blind man had seen a cripple run like the wind. And from there she would jump to a different game, the one filled with magical images that said today is a Sunday the pipe tree's fun day, the pipe is made of mud and beats on the jug, the jug is truly swell and beats on the bell, the bell is made of gold and beats on the troll, the troll is very brave and beats on the knave, the knave is very frail and falls into the pail, the pail becomes a swirl, it's the end of the world.

Three tragic tigers. The rat and the robe of the reign of Rome.

Mother.

Maria Inês slowly opened her eyes.

She sat on the edge of the bed and looked at Maria Inês's manicured nails and looked at her own bitten-down nails.

My mother had very blue eyes, Maria Inês said. Eduarda nodded in agreement. Eduarda never knew Otacília, who had died before she was born.

Maria Inês looked at her daughter. They were both thinking about the farm and Clarice, the sister and the aunt Clarice.

Are you sure you wouldn't rather go with your father?

I'm sure, answered Eduarda.

Maria Inês closed her dark eyes again. She took a deep breath and thought once more that it just might be possible.

A tall-short fat-skinny man sitting down-standing up on a stone-wooden bench.

Who is that relative of your father's that works in films? The half-bald one.

A guy named Artur. He's a second cousin.

Like me.

They smiled.

He started to pour his heart out to me.

He separated from his wife.

Eduarda did not need anyone to suggest that her father had been seeing cousin Artur's ex-wife. She didn't need to be a fortune-teller or seer to know that her parents did not kiss each other anymore. Her mother had an occasional lover in another country, an old med school classmate; they met once a year or something to that effect. Her father was seeing cousin Artur's ex-wife.

But Eduarda did not know, for example, about a young Venetian. *Sitting down-standing up on a stone-wooden bench at the Café Florian and the pigeons in the Piazza San Marco carpeting the ground. The stinking canals smelling good. The sweet-smelling stench, like the odor of cow dung at the farm. Venice, a dream, a nightmare.*

I've had too much to drink. When are they all leaving?

It's still early, Mom. We haven't even served dinner yet. Do you want me to get you some coffee?

Maria Inês nodded and said I want some strong coffee, coffee and a Coke, please.

She had heard that combination kept truck drivers awake. Others preferred cocaine, like Clarice. In another lifetime, before the clinic.

While Eduarda went to the kitchen, Maria Inês rolled over on her side and looked at the picture frame sitting on her bedside table. There were various photographs cut to form a mosaic. Eduarda as a small child playing in the dunes at Cabo Frio, by the sea. Eduarda and her inseparable friends all spiffed up in their uniforms for the first day of the school year, impeccably straight parts in their combed hair, new clothes, sparkling white sneakers and fearful smiles. *Mrs.* Clarice in 1970, dressed up as a bride. Maria Inês and Clarice at the ages of seven and eleven, respectively, before the courses of nature were inverted and the seasons no longer seemed natural.

Maria Inês thought that her daughter was almost pretty. Long-limbed, expressive features, with calm words and fluid ideas. She had light blue eyes, but not like Otacília's aquamarine blue eyes. Eduarda was uncomplicated, airy, a person of simple gestures.

She returned to the bedroom carrying a small tray with a steaming coffee server. A cup and saucer. No sugar. And also a red, black, silver can of Coca-Cola.

There you go, Mom.

Everything swirled around Maria Inês, closing her eyes made it worse because the bed began to sink into a quicksand ground and rock like a boat in rough seas.

When will we leave? asked Eduarda.

My vacation at the hospital starts on the second. We'll wait for your father to travel. We can go the next day.

How long will we stay?

As long as we want. One day, two, ten days, a month.

Or the rest of our lives?

Would you like that?

Maybe.

There's someone there I intend to see again, besides my sister.

Eduarda nodded and didn't risk asking any questions. Maria Inês was drunk and might say more than she'd want to hear. At any rate, Eduarda valued that certain distance, a healthy distance between mother and daughter. Each one in control of her own secrets.

A little more coffee?

Maria Inês had some more. Then she got off the bed as if she'd just had an operation, and her movements gave the impression that her whole body ached. She smoothed down her dress and ran her fingers through her short hair and opened her eyes wide at herself in the mirror and because of this gesture was reminded of Little Red Riding Hood, what big eyes you have, Grandmother.

She returned to the living room, and João Miguel whispered people were beginning to ask where you were.

Maria Inês softly caressed his wounded wrist, so softly he barely felt her touch.

I hope this gets well soon, she said, and then went over to the sound system to play the trio again. Horn, violin and piano. The beardless, long-haired rocker in the Guns N' Roses t-shirt shot her a glance of frank disapproval.

At the state hospital where Maria Inês worked there were people who had never actually seen a tennis racquet, who did not have the slightest notion of the existence of the canals in Venice, and who would laugh out loud if they were to see the prices on certain menus. That much for a steak? You have to be kidding me, Doctor.

There, Maria Inês was the Doctor. Although it had been almost twenty years, she still had trouble recognizing herself being addressed as such, a form of address that had never inflated her ego. She was not a good physician, but she liked the people she saw. She was a dermatologist. Fungus, acne, scabies, psoriasis, Hansen's disease, skin cancer.

Her boss had once classified her as a typical bourgeois who did a bit of social work between an afternoon tea and a manicure, as if she were giving coins to beggars at traffic lights, without rolling down the windows of her car very much, of course, so as not to risk being robbed. That same boss was relieved of his duties a month later, when his signature appeared on padded invoices for surgical supplies, an everyday occurrence, which unfortunately, at the time, leaked to the press. Her boss was transferred to another sector.

Otacília and Afonso Olímpio had already died when Maria Inês received her diploma from the Universidade Federal in 1979. Among the other graduates with real or fake emerald rings on their fingers and diplomas in their hands was a young man by the name of

Bernardo Águas, who had a beautiful baritone voice and eventually abandoned medicine for a career as a singer. It was in his arms that Maria Inês found herself from time to time, perhaps once or twice a year. Whenever he was in Rio, Bernardo Águas called her, and they would drink gin and tonics in some bar that overlooked the ocean and listen to music in the car and end the afternoon in the apartment he kept in Rio, having perfunctory sex that had nothing to do with love and very little to do with friendship. It was like an exercise that afforded them each a specific advantage or the illusion of one.

Maria Inês associated Bernardo Águas with afternoons covered in sea mist, with mild gin and tonic binges, and with those gentle Renaissance and Baroque songs he interpreted so well: Monteverdi, John Dowland, Marc-Antoine Charpentier, Purcell, Gesualdo, Lully, songs that didn't seem to go with his heavyset body, his gray beard, his hair pulled back in a ponytail, a la Don Juan. Dr. Jekyll and Mr. Hyde. Maria Inês felt seduced by both, or maybe even more by the harshness of that relationship, by its melancholic superficiality, by its fake, sweet words.

She knew that Bernardo Águas had other occasional lovers in Rio, in other cities, that he liked having a worldwide harem. He did not try to hide the fact and had actually mentioned, on one occasion: have you ever thought if I bought a map of the world and started to mark all the places where I've had a girlfriend? And he began to name them: Rio, São Paulo, Curitiba, London, Louvain, Paris, Milan . . .

Asshole, Maria Inês thought, but kissed him all the same. At his side she became a colored pin on a world map. And not having a name was, at times, comfortable.

In the early hours of the twenty-fifth of December, after the family exchanged colorful presents and after more Coca-Colas-with-coffee alternated with wine, Maria Inês lay down to sleep and dreamed about Bernardo Águas: an erotic, unimportant dream. She never dreamed about Tomás.

The next morning, when they awoke, João Miguel did not have as bad a hangover as Maria Inês. But he, as well, had fabricated his own dreams and was still wrapped up in them. He sat down and looked at the odd acrylic lilies, blatantly artificial, with their white stems, bunched together in a twisted vase. The morning heat was sticky and lethargic. João Miguel noticed it somewhere in the back of his head, but not even the bloated air managed to bother him.

Life was so colorful and exciting, like a plate of Indian food or a ride on a roller coaster or a piece of velvet embroidered with sequins and beads. Or like the recently separated Luciana's arms that smelled of talcum powder, with golden hairs sprinkled about. João Miguel had dreamed about her and had woken up as hard as a teenager. He could have reached out and touched Maria Inês's half-exposed shoulder, but he could also leave things as they were. He opted for the latter alternative and went to the living room to continue his dream.

In a nearby apartment a child had received his present from his wealthy Santa Claus, an electronic toy making noise that could be faintly heard in the distance. But it was loud enough to disturb João Miguel and jerk him out of his daydreaming. In front of the sound system was the Brahms trio, which he put on to play.

Eduarda came into the living room and sat on the floor, close to him, and commented with feigned impatience man, that's the only thing we've heard in this house since yesterday.

She started to eat some dried dates and figs and apricots that were left over from the party.

Are you sure you don't want to come? he asked. On the trip, with me. There's still time to get you a ticket, if you change your mind.

Eduarda said I'm sure. I want to visit Aunt Clarice.

And she threw him a challenging glance. She wanted to make it clear that she preferred her Aunt Clarice to Grandfather Azzopardi. Offend him. For no good reason.

João Miguel raised his eyebrows and shrugged.

Are you going to have a tennis lesson tomorrow? she asked.

I don't think so. My wrist still hurts a little.

Eduarda popped a few more dried apricots into her mouth. She loved that color. She felt light tart pricks on her tongue. She wore a short blouse that exposed her navel, with its small silver ring. João Miguel stretched out his arm to the plate with dried fruits and picked up a date.

The afternoon is cool and pleasant. The cypress trees smell wonderful and are full of those small green seeds children like to collect. It is that precise, subtle moment in which the sun has disappeared behind the hills but has not yet taken away all its light.

Nine years old is just another way of saying: promises. Life is a vast seam of precise moments, a telescope set up below the vast night sky, or a microscope that examines a drop of water.

Oh, the cypress trees smell so good! And this young child's body, how fluidly and easily it runs! *Everything matters*. Everything has a function, even little green cypress seeds: later the children will turn them into an alternative monetary unit and negotiate.

How much does that mud cake with chopped daisy icing cost?

Five cypress seeds.

One smile, two smiles, three smiles. One tiger, two tigers, three tragic tigers. This is an era in which time *has a smell*. It just might be possible to make a *time perfume*. Of course this nine-year-old girl has already thought of that.

She runs, alone and happy—the most authentic happiness, the kind that doesn't need to be recognized—among the cypress trees. Each cypress tree has a body and a face, each one has a soul, she has no doubt of that. That is why she asks their permission to take their green seeds. The sky is so weightless, looking at it reveals a precise notion of infinity. But infinity can die in a second.

Or: infinity can die in a second that will freeze and last forever, the opposite of infinity. A moment that grabs childhood by the neck, immobilizes it on the ground with an arm lock and crushes its fragile lungs until it suffocates. A moment that rips the fetus from the womb and interrupts its life, dries up the roots of the cypress trees, and crushes underfoot mud cakes with chopped daisy icing.

The hall in the house smells like freshly waxed floors. She walks on the tips of her toes, she thinks by doing so she is already training to be a ballerina, she wants to be a ballerina when she grows up, and she has a doll (a present from her godmother) with a net tutu, ballet slippers, a hairnet on its hair, and a tiara with small white stones that she thinks are real diamonds. They must be, her godmother is very rich. Her cupped hands hold several dozen cypress seeds. She, too, is rich, as rich as her godmother.

The door to the bedroom is half-open. The bedroom door is not usually half-open. Something moves inside, a monster with only one eye that drools and grunts and grits its horrendous jaws. The monster that devours childhoods. The half-open door reveals a scene that could be quite beautiful: the pale volume that the nine-year-old girl does not yet know in her own body. A breast, all made of curves, without any aggressive angles, accompanied by a shoulder so rounded, by an arm so soft, and a stomach as smooth as paper. She looks, fascinated, as a masculine hand draws near and reaches that delicate piece of anatomy, while rigid fingers fondle the base of the breast, and then slide along the vertiginous valley until they reach the nipple and hold it for a moment between the thumb and the index finger. As if they were winding a wristwatch.

She sees. Afterwards, the cypress seeds fall from her cupped hands. She wants to close her eyes and go back in time. At that instant the sun begins to steal away its light but the night that is begotten is different from all others: it is a night that is stillborn. The seeds roll along the recently waxed floor and a tear of pain and fear rolls down the face of the girl who now flees, still on tiptoes. No longer, however, because she wants to be a ballerina. Now she wants to avoid being heard, she does not want them to know she knows.

The cypress seeds lie scattered on the floor.

Vivid Red Roses

When the first butterfly of the morning opened its wings and took flight over the quarry, which was off limits for her daughters, Otacília had already been up for quite a while. She had watched the dawn of the new day and the gradual disappearance of the shadows that covered the valley like a carpet.

At three, four o'clock in the morning, the world turned into something akin to an interval, things either did not yet exist or had ceased to exist. To be awake, to walk about the house and the front porch was to temporarily interrupt oneself, witness life inside out. With the sun, the spell was gradually broken, and the world sat up straight and opened its eyes, and she, Otacília, grieved.

On that summer morning, hot and humid, a decision was beginning to form, and it was a decision of peace, although overdue. Even though there was now no way of knowing if it would be worthwhile.

Around seven-thirty Afonso Olímpio woke up and went to the table, where the maid had already placed the milk, fresh from the cow that very morning, and the coffee and sugar, the cornbread, the butter, the cured cheese, and the papaya preserves. Among the many morning sounds, the distinct singing of the rufous-bellied thrushes and the great kiskadees stood out.

He said good morning to Otacília, who was leaning out the

window and holding a cup of coffee into which she had secretly poured a shot of brandy.

She answered good morning.

He cracked all the bones in his hands in one fluid movement and sighed deeply while he leisurely studied the breakfast table.

Today we'll surely sell the rest of the beans, the thirty sacks, he said, pleased.

He still looked so much like the Afonso Olímpio who had discovered Otacília, single and without hope, at her parents' home, the same man she had married on the happiest and most unreal day of her life. A man from Minas Gerais with the ways of Minas Gerais, few words and precise gestures.

It was very easy to believe in Afonso Olímpio and his mild manners and his quiet Sunday afternoons with a book on his lap and a pipe in his mouth. Five days or five years of living together, the general impression was he didn't have any tricks hidden up his sleeves. And that he was even somewhat mediocre or limited. Afonso Olímpio seemed to be made of mere appearances, and was, without a doubt, essentially good, the way only mild-mannered people could be.

He was small, thin. He didn't even look like much. He could be reduced to the sweet-smelling tobacco he slowly consumed.

Tomorrow I need to go to the doctor, Otacília reminded him, and he nodded. He would take her in the car, which rarely left the garage (he ran the motor a little every other day so the battery wouldn't go dead), and hold her by the forearm. But no one must know, especially the girls. All the codes had to be maintained, even if on another level everything was defilement. Otacília took a deep breath, adjusted the tone of her voice and said, in a calm manner, I've decided to send Clarice to Rio de Janeiro. To study.

Afonso Olímpio finished chewing the piece of cornbread that he had just bitten off. Then he took a sip of coffee and wiped the corner of his mouth with his napkin. He didn't look at his wife, he almost never looked her in the eye. He coughed. It was a polite, repressed cough, and he covered his mouth with one hand while the other held the coffee cup. Outside, the kiskadees and thrushes were unperturbed and continued to sing ferociously.

What is the reason for this? he asked and was as calm as ever, low voice, velvety words.

Otacília made a vague gesture with her hands and said for her future. She can't study here. In Rio de Janeiro she can go to high school, learn French or music.

I don't know if I think that's a good idea, he said.

She and I have talked about it, lied Otacília. I've already talked to my Aunt Berenice, who can take her in, she lied again.

You didn't lose any time, he said.

Otacília fell silent. She joined her hands the way she did to pray.

So you've already talked to your daughter about all this, Afonso Olímpio repeated, and Otacília nodded.

They had forgotten to wind the grandfather clock and the pendulum hung lazy and silent. Otacília was afraid. Afonso Olímpio, in a certain sense, as well. The kiskadees and thrushes sang outside with their clear, crystalline voices.

She excused herself and went to Clarice's bedroom and turned the door handle. The door was never locked because in that house the girls were forbidden to lock themselves in their rooms. She didn't find her in bed. She continued down the hallway and opened the door to Maria Inês's room, and there were the two girls asleep in the same bed, head to toe for more space.

Maria Inês was sleeping with her mouth open and her head turned towards the pillow. On the bedside table there was a glass of water covered with a saucer (Maria Inês worried she might swallow a drowned mosquito during the night) and the ballet doll that was her greatest treasure. On the floor, next to the bed, were two pairs of cloth slippers, the larger yellow pair and the smaller blue and white pair. A black beetle dragged itself across the top of the chest of drawers, its feet covered in dust. Maria Inês would help it when she woke up, clean it, release it back into the garden.

Otacília did not call Clarice, she said nothing, and closed the door again.

In the living room, she could see Afonso Olímpio's profile at the table. He was silent, and his impassive face held nothing. She sat down at the table again to eat half a piece of bread with butter, even though she wasn't hungry, simply because that was what she ate every morning.

They had already wound up the clock when Clarice came in for breakfast. She always woke up before Maria Inês, without exception, and never appeared like her sister, with uncombed hair, in a nightgown, smelling of sleep: Clarice always got fully dressed, her hair pulled back, her shoes on.

Good morning, she said in her soft voice, and she sat down, filled her coffee cup with milk, sugar, and coffee, cut a piece of cornbread.

Afonso Olímpio said your mother told me you two have been talking about your going to study in Rio. That you agree.

She looked at her coffee cup and pretended to skim the cream off the top with her spoon. A tremor ran down her arms and reached her hands, exposing her. She nodded yes.

Just then Maria Inês arrived, not quite awake, rubbing her eyes with closed fists. And Otacília wanted to end that game, get it all over with, so she said, before the good mornings, as if everything was practically decided: guess what, Maria Inês, what good news. Your sister is going to Rio de Janeiro to study.

A monster that roamed through the house emitted a deep grunt that the father, the mother, and the two girls heard, but for each one of them it had a different face, and its voice, a distinct and secret tone.

Otacília did not bring up the subject for the rest of the day, and no one ever knew she had a horse saddled in the late afternoon and went by herself to Jabuticabais to call Berenice, her maiden aunt in the big city, and ask her a favor that could not be denied.

They were digging up clay at the river bank. Clarice liked the sensation of the small grains entering under her fingernails. She had three friends: Damião, a small ten-year-old black boy who was always butting heads with Maria Inês. Lina, black and beautiful, unaware of her own developing body and the stares she provoked in men. And Casimiro, as blonde as a Baroque angel, with a belly almost always bloated with worms. Lina went to school, but was so far behind she still barely knew how to read. Casimiro and Damião didn't go because they helped out in the fields.

They were her friends, but Clarice didn't say anything about the story that she herself did not quite understand: Rio de Janeiro. To study. Study what? Live where? With whom? Why? She knew why.

Lina, Damião, and Casimiro helped her dig up mud at the river bank, clay that she would later use in sculptures that gave form to dreams and strived to compose things worthy of her beliefs. She was barefoot and could feel, beneath her thick soles, the small stones of the riverbank. Damião's feet were full of chigoe fleas.

Go by my house later, Damião, tell them to call me. I'll pull those bugs out for you.

And the boy opened wide his incredibly black eyes, filled with unspoken gratitude. Clarice often did that, with a flame-sterilized needle she would open the nodule where the parasite was lodged, under the skin. She would then remove the puss and apply iodine. Damião was always getting chigoe fleas. He always had on some half-torn flip-flops. The only closed shoes he owned were a pair of very old, loose, high-topped shoes some landowner had discarded and which he saved for church on Sundays.

Lina's hair was a pitiful fright. She still did not realize she had the breasts of a woman. She wore a very small white blouse, worn-out from so much use. She seemed more childlike than the boy Damião. Clarice had once overheard a conversation in which the supposition was expressed: Lina was a little *retarded*. Lina loved to plait Clarice's hair and liked to sit Maria Inês in her lap like a baby.

One day I'm going to have a daughter, she said, and I'm going to name her Maria Inês Clarice.

Lina's father was continually getting drunk and passing out along the road. Her mother, who washed and ironed for a living, always had a bundle of clothes balanced miraculously on top of her head.

Sit there on that rock and stay still, Lina.

What for?

I'm going to make a sculpture of you.

While Clarice molded the clay, Casimiro ate a little of that same clay, when no one was looking. It was a bright, clear day, botflies were buzzing against the aching blue of the sky and low-flying dragonflies skimmed the surface of the river. Two of them appeared to be stuck together.

Look at that, pointed Damião, mischievously, and they all thought the coupling of the insects was comical, except for Clarice.

Dogs are even funnier, Casimiro assured them, and Lina said oh no, you haven't seen horses.

What I've never seen is people, sighed Damião, but Clarice interrupted and said let's stop this talk right now!

Everyone got quiet. She regretted her rude tone of voice and added it's because I'm making a sculpture and you're distracting me with all that silly talk. But her words were already painted in sadness. A small ragged cloud defaced the sky and vultures began to circle a nearby hill. On the ground, next to Clarice, an immense tick appeared, which she crushed with her foot. Then she tried to concentrate on her hands, on Lina's body that the sculpture should portray as it was, quirks of a child in the shape of a woman.

At that moment the small ragged cloud wandering through the sky moved right in front of the sun, and it grew dark. Lina's sculpture took on deep set eyes, later, when Clarice tried to finish it by candlelight, in her room.

A week later Otacília called her in the middle of the night. It was past two.

I want to show you the moon, Clarice. It just came up.

They both went out into the yard barefoot, in silence. A fat yellow moon rose behind the pine grove and transformed the trees into enormous black skeletons. The air was motionless and hot. Mother and daughter did not hold hands. There was an owl hooting nearby, bats whistled and flew rapidly among the trees, a black trail of ants crossed the path between a bush and a swollen ant hill.

We won't be seeing each other very much, said Otacília, and Clarice knew she was referring to Rio.

Between them there were no confessions, no exchanges of caresses. Clarice was surprised by her mother's resolve to send her away. Because if it was all so underground, if it was all so secret.

Besides that, I'm sick, Otacília added, breaking another rule.

What do you have?

They don't know yet. You don't need to worry about that, you have your own affairs. Then she added: and you don't need to tell Maria Inês.

They did not look at each other.

Who am I going to live with?

With my Aunt Berenice. She has an apartment in the Flamengo neighborhood, close to the beach.

Clarice bit her lips. Maria Inês is going to miss me, she said.

Don't be silly. Maria Inês has her friends here, and that cousin João Miguel comes here on all his vacations. You can write each other.

Maybe she can come visit, every once in a while.

Otacília sighed, she seemed weak, a dry leaf hanging precariously onto a branch, which the slightest breeze pulls off and tosses to its fate.

Perhaps, she answered.

Clarice did not take her eyes off the moon.

The Americans are going to send men up there, she said, pointing, but immediately drew back her hand because Casimiro had warned her that pointing at the moon would cause a wart to grow on the tip of her finger.

Otacília shook her head and said they'll never make it.

Clarice crossed her fingers, *they have to make it*. To be launched into space, leave the planet, step on virgin land. It would be like being born again. She remembered it was her birthday, she was turning fifteen years old, that age when girls had beautiful parties during which they smiled without stopping, tucked into full pink dresses, and danced *The Blue Danube* with their proud fathers. She had not wanted a party.

What disease do you have, Mother?

I already told you not to think about that.

Clarice wanted to hug her. She wanted to stroke her hair. The monster that didn't sleep let out a moan of pain and tripped on some cypress seeds that had fallen in the hallway—those had been swept up long ago, of course, and no one ever suspected what had been planted with those dead seeds. But Clarice did not have a way of sweeping them out of her memory.

Otacília said: in a few years, when she's a little older, Maria Inês could also go study in Rio de Janeiro. Who knows? Let's go in now.

Clarice obeyed her and thought about going to the big city throughout a night of insomnia, during which she uninterruptedly heard the monster scratching at the door of her room. And suddenly she wanted to go, she wanted it very badly, at that very instant, quickly, in spite of everything, in spite of Maria Inês, Otacília's illness, in spite of Casimiro and Lina and Damião: get away. If she were American, she could conceivably go to the moon. And breathe in the immense universe and finally feel that nothing else mattered, that everything disintegrated like the slow-moving night at dawn, that everything dried up like a puddle under the sun.

The wind switched directions and that meant rain. Maria Inês and her second cousin João Miguel were tying a swing made of a rope and an old tire onto the lowest branch of the mango tree. Clarice could see them from her bedroom window while, alone, she put her clothes and belongings on top of the bed. João Miguel and Maria Inês seemed so small, they *were* so small. Maria Inês had her hair pulled back into two long plaits and the wind turned them for an instant into two enchanted serpents. The air did not smell good.

Clarice had taken a bath after Otacília and had noticed a lock of her mother's hair that had fallen in the shower, close to the drain, a big lock. The water had shaped it into a perfect roll. Since it was hot, Clarice wanted to bathe in cold water, but there the water came from the underground spring and it was *really* cold, too cold, and made her lips turn blue. She got completely dressed in the bathroom, felt her own icy forearms with her hands, and realized that the small mirror smiled back at her. The wasps were beginning to build a new house on the window.

Now, she made her selections. She was vaguely cheerful, as if she had recuperated some sort of promise, some certainty that reality was materializing *this* way, and not *that* way. She found a dress she had completely forgotten about, it was too short for her now. She could give it to Maria Inês. And that pair of shoes, too tight. The wind rattled a window somewhere in the house. Then Clarice found her white dress, brand new, which she never used because she didn't think it looked good on her. Maria Inês could save it until she was older, and, who knows, maybe someday practice her ballet steps in it.

That night there was going to be a going-away dinner (which

was also a discreet commemoration of Clarice's recent fifteenth birthday) and her parents had invited half a dozen relatives who lived in Jabuticabais and also the neighboring landowner, his wife, and his son, a slight boy named Ilton Xavier, who had a ridiculous adolescent moustache and liked to pretend that he noticed all the women's legs and asses. He would later become Clarice's husband, and then Clarice's ex-husband. And later, much later, would buy an expensive red pickup.

Clarice had a few books. *Pollyanna. Pollyanna Grows Up. Model Little Girls.* And things of that sort. She intended to leave them for Maria Inês although she knew her sister wouldn't read them. Clarice filled the two suitcases and wrapped up her papers into a brown-paper package. That was it. She would have been happy to take fewer things, even less, leave all the dead skin behind, if possible. But Otacília had ordered her to fill two suitcases.

Lina was in the kitchen. She had come to help make the sweets. And Otacília, who was in charge, looking shrunken and thin, worked sitting on a bench. Clarice came in to see if she could help and discovered that the kitchen had been transformed into a factory, where powerful aromas mixed together and an array of colors was on display. The creamed caramel bubbled in a large, shallow pan. Three beautiful compote dishes were on top of the table, one still empty, the other two, respectively, green with the unripe papaya compote, orange with the pumpkin and coconut compote. Lina was paring guavas and eating the peels; she had tied her hair back with a scarf that had belonged to Otacília ages before. It still had vestiges of the roses that had once been flashy, vivid, red.

Have you finished my sculpture? she asked Clarice, and added, spontaneously: won't you give it to me as a present before you go away?

Clarice had hidden her sculptures in the stable, at the top of a big rustic cabinet that was only used to keep old objects, junk, worthless items, broken tools that would never be fixed.

Sure, I'll give it to you as a present, if you'd like. But you're much prettier than it is.

Lina laughed. Early tomorrow morning I'll come tell you good-bye, you give me the sculpture.

It's a deal. And I want you to study a lot so you can write me letters.

Lina half-heartedly pouted, but agreed, okay, I'll study.

Promise?

And she nodded with her mouth full of guava peels.

The night fell cloudy and dirty, full of dust and vague thoughts in the air. As Ilton Xavier arrived with a bouquet of flowers, well-dressed, precocious seducer, Lina ate a plate of rice and beans and pork loin in the kitchen. After her last forkful she began to sob.

Don't do that, Clarice said. We're going to be friends forever. I'm going to be in your wedding and I'll also be your daughter's god-mother.

Lina drank a sip of coffee, then said good-bye, still red-eyed.

I'll come tomorrow morning. Real early.

And I'll give you the sculpture.

She washed her hands and mouth at the outside sink, the cement tank that had been dated and signed by the stonemason as if it, too, were a sculpture. Then she left and Clarice watched her draw away, her white clothes, the scarf with memories of vivid red roses.

During dinner, everything seemed so dangerously casual. As always. The smiles, the words, and the glances. Otacília smiled, impenetrable, feverish. Afonso Olímpio smiled, small, scary. The pendulum clock smiled beneath a new layer of wood polish and marked the seconds like a metronome.

They ate, they drank, they talked. An uncle from Jabuticabais told a joke, which Otacília considered improper and listened to with a frown. The uncle changed the subject and started to talk about the price of beef on the hoof.

Not far from there was Lina, on the road, in the depth of the moonless night.

And Ilton Xavier invented a sentence in code for Clarice. He wanted to win her heart, perhaps even steal a kiss with which he could predict the future.

And Maria Inês, unaware of its complicated name, shared a palindrome with João Miguel: Neil, a trap! Sid is part alien, she said.

What about it?

It's the same thing backwards.

Lina was on her way home, she smelled sweaty and felt an odd sadness gnawing at her heart. She *would* learn to read and write correctly. She *would* write those letters.

João Miguel got a piece of paper to write down the sentence and see if it was, in fact, the same thing backwards. *Neil, a trap! Sid is part alien. neila trap si diS part a lieN*. Each child was allowed one glass of punch. They just weren't allowed coffee, because afterwards they wouldn't sleep.

The man came out of the bushes, from behind a grove of cypress trees. He was waiting for her. He knew a lot of things, even though he wasn't from those parts. He knew a lot of things and was waiting for her, for Lina, and came out like a specter from behind a grove of cypress trees. The black night made him dark and uniform, even his hat and eyes—two-dimensional, as if he was not a person, but rather a sketch on a piece of paper.

Lina did not scream, because his first gesture, rapid and calculated, was to cover her mouth with a hand that was too strong, exaggeratedly strong. No one needed to be that strong to cover Lina's mouth, to dominate her, and keep her from crying out.

It lasted half an hour and meant very little. Practically nothing. It was only then that the rain began to fall, impartial, merciless.

They whispered, the following morning:

I always thought a tragedy like this would happen to that girl.

She didn't have any sense.

Maybe she brought it on herself. Didn't you notice how she dressed?

Sort of provocatively.

Sort of shamelessly.

Otacília and Afonso Olímpio declared Lina's death *forbidden*, and had Maria Inês and João Miguel go inside, and ordered the taxi driver, who was waiting for Clarice (to take her to the Jabuticabais bus station, where she would catch the bus to Nova Friburgo, and from there to Rio de Janeiro), to start the car.

An odd, unreal steam rose off the still-damp ground. Clarice faced her parents, as she hugged Lina's statue. They took their time looking at each other. Everything around them was such confusion that it seemed like Fat Tuesday with its high-pitched horns, masked merrymakers, showers of streamers and confetti. An inside-out Carnival. And Lina was just a coincidence.

Maria Inês had a fight with João Miguel, who did not want to leave her side: hey, leave me alone for a minute! and took off in a run, followed by her long, dark braids. She ran to watch the car that was leaving, taking Clarice to Rio de Janeiro. And in the midst of so many electrical currents that ran through her, she found space to improvise a semblance of a prayer for her sister.

Clarice had climbed into the purring car in the middle of a multitude of people coming and going, arriving on horseback, arriving by car, contorting their faces or crying openly. Somewhere lay Lina who was not Lina anymore, who had been stripped of whatever made her Lina, and Clarice squeezed her eyes shut and was overcome by a violent memory that had nothing to do with Lina.

It's over. But what did *over* mean? Would her childhood undergo a revolution, in her memory, and *return to normal*? The thrushes and the kiskadees continued to sing. The car was moving slowly and the driver said something about the crime. It sounded confused to Clarice, she could not distinguish a single word in that amorphous mumble of sounds.

She felt nauseated and asked the driver please stop the car for a minute. She was not thinking about Lina, not specifically. She opened the door and vomited onto the dirt road, the same dirt road where her friend had been raped and murdered, those were the forbidden words. There on the ground, muddy from the rain, was Lina's scarf, the scarf where one day it had been possible to distinguish vivid red roses, flashy, explicit. Clarice looked back and saw the thin, small shape of her father in the distance.

"Si ch'io vorrei morire . . ."

Always her, always Maria Inês. Who had magically been capable of tattooing herself, of branding herself as cattle are branded, on Tomás's existence. And on Clarice's existence. A shimmering rainbow in the sky after rain. The after-image of the sun in the eyes. The smoke that hovers in the air after blowing out a match, the aroma of incense that outlives the stick. A faded scarf.

On that hot evening at the farm, the eve of Maria Inês's arrival after so many years, Clarice said to Tomás, as she carved swirls out of a piece of wood with a pocket knife: I had a friend once. Her name was Abrilina, but to us she was just Lina.

Tomás stroked the hair of the dog lying next to him.

She died over thirty years ago, said Clarice, and she told him the story of Lina, who was merely a coincidence, a raw, everyday death quickly forgotten.

At that going-away dinner, also commemorative of Clarice's fifteenth birthday, Maria Inês had shot her a piercing look, her eyes ablaze. A look that Clarice never forgot.

Always her, always Maria Inês. In a manner askew, immune to time, immune to distance and to any attempt to keep her away. Maria Inês was the warped mirror capable of revealing the worst. Clarice and also Tomás could never forgive her, nor thank her enough.

Clarice arrived in Rio de Janeiro in 1965 and knocked on her great-aunt Berenice's door laden with her two suitcases and the brown paper package. Great-Aunt Berenice did not ask any questions and simply showed her to the bedroom that was ready and waiting for her.

It was a bedroom with windows that, instead of opening onto Maria Inês's pigtails on her swing, opened onto an asphalt street and apartment buildings and, to her left, the row of trees in the Aterro Park and the sea beyond. She would live in that city bedroom for five years and from there she would go directly to the small church in Jabuticabais where Ilton Xavier would be waiting at the altar while a multitude of people bumped elbows to see her, the Bride.

The previous evening, during dinner, Ilton Xavier had yanked a promise from Clarice to write him. And snatched a fleeting kiss, in the hall that separated the living room from the bedrooms, pressing her against the rough stucco wall.

Now her stomach ached, her head ached. She mentioned it to her great-aunt and her own voice startled her, as if it had been silent for many years.

Would you have anything for me to take, please?

Go lie down, take off those hot clothes, and put on something more comfortable. I'll bring you some medicine and something to eat.

Just a glass of milk would be fine.

But her great-aunt, who had selective hearing, fixed a tray with soup, bread, butter, lemonade, pudding. And she spoke in her creamy voice while Clarice ate, talking about all the things they could do the next week. There were so many pretty places to see in Rio de Janeiro. And handsome young men, too.

We're going to put you in a good school. And what else? Find a piano teacher? French? There's so much to do when you're fifteen.

Great-Aunt Berenice closed the curtains and went out, saying now rest.

Clarice lay down on the bed that had a soft mattress and clean sheets. Right there, at that exact moment, without realizing it, she began the enterprise that would keep her feverishly busy for the long years to follow: forget who Clarice was.

Forget. Scrape out her soul with a fine-edged blade, a surgical scalpel, and *forget*. When Clarice softly stroked the hair on her arm, the contact hurt. Through the closed curtains a sepia luminosity, aged, homogenized the room.

She got off the bed. In one of her suitcases there was a small quantity of damp clay enfolded in plastic and then in newspaper. She carefully unwrapped the clay, smoothed out the newspaper, folded it over once and spread it out on the floor. Forget. Maybe Clarice could sculpt that, but nothing took shape. Not that she was lacking in ideas, but it was as if they had no face or shape. In the meantime, the light of day leisurely abandoned the room.

Maria Inês's eyes were no longer on fire. She applied mascara to her eyelashes and quickly brushed her short hair that didn't really need combing. She flushed the toilet and watched the blue perfumed liquid go down with the water in an eddy. She then looked to see if her eye makeup was done properly and removed a spot of mascara that had stuck to the corner of her left eyelid. She enjoyed making up her eyes to appear deep-set, immersed in a long tunnel of long eyelashes covered with mascara and eyelids decorated with a light layer of brown eye shadow and a touch of black eyeliner. She hid the circles under her eyes with concealer. A drop of foundation. There was no other makeup on the rest of her face.

She checked to make sure she had gotten her keys. They were there, inside her purse, organized in the leather key case that had a metal plate with two random engraved initials. How silly, a key case with initials that are not even mine, thought Maria Inês, and imagined a plate inscribed with: M. I. A. How silly, as well.

It was time to leave. João Miguel's suitcases were already in the car, she had offered to take him to the airport. Silently, Eduarda appeared in the living room, she had on a pair of sneakers, it was obvious she would also go to the airport, although a few hours earlier she had declared with indifference that she wouldn't.

Dad's not ready yet, she said.

Of course not, he wasn't ready because he had scheduled a tennis lesson for the late afternoon (the injured wrist now entirely well) and then he had stayed there a little longer, drinking tequila sunrises at the bar next to the pool. It didn't upset Maria Inês now. It seemed as if things were already taking a new direction.

It had not upset her, but half an hour later, as she drove, she put on a certain recording of a madrigal by Claudio Monteverdi, with the participation of a certain baritone named Bernardo Águas.

Si ch'io vorrei morire
Ora ch'io baccio, amore,
La bella bocca del mio amato core.
[Yes, I would gladly die
as I kiss, even now, my love,
the sweet lips of my beloved.]

They drove along the Lagoa Rodrigo de Freitas, Rio's South Zone lagoon, now dark, in the middle of which rose an immense Christmas tree, all lit up. The entire city was overtaken by the vice of the minuscule made-in-Taiwan lights—trees, store and building façades, flower beds, windows, everything glittered. They entered the tunnel and emerged in the São Cristóvão neighborhood and then caught the Linha Vermelha expressway where the speed limit was fifty-five miles per hour but all the cars did sixty, seventy, sometimes hitting eighty miles an hour. In a few minutes they would be crossing the exact opposite of the Lagoa, a stinking mangrove thicket where low-income housing projects peeked out from behind billboards advertising cellular phones. They passed by the Hospital Universitário. And, at last, Ilha do Governador and the international airport.

Maria Inês felt a shiver that didn't mean very much as she recalled an occasion when she had gone to meet Bernardo Águas at the airport. He had arrived to spend only a week in Brazil. They had gone straight from the airport to a no-tell motel out on Avenida Brasil.

It was not particularly good to remember that, but it was not exactly bad, either. Maria Inês looked for a parking place and the music was no longer playing in the car. But she continued to sing *Si ch'io vorrei morire* with bad pronunciation. It was a madrigal and the other voices were missing. But it didn't matter. She wasn't much of a singer.

She fiddled with her key case in her purse and thought about the metal plate again. The executive class began to board. A multitude of passengers would soon be elbowing one another in tourist class for possession of the baggage compartments. Here, João Miguel was a passenger in the executive class. Out there, he would carry a Brazilian passport that always inspired distrust in first-world customs officials.

Maria Inês felt good about not boarding. Glad she would not be seeing the *vecchio* Azzopardi again. Not drink Chianti at the table of his beautiful villa. Not be the false loverwife, who once had not been all that false, of the prosperous João Miguel, who once had not been all that prosperous.

They said good-bye with a hug that could mean so much, forgive me, forget me, I don't forgive you. I made a mistake. We made mistakes. Don't say anything, please, okay? *We can start all over again*. Look, you'd better hurry. Drive carefully. I'll call you. Call me. Don't bother. Leave and get it over with.

Back in Leblon, Maria Inês told Eduarda good night and went to pack her bags.

Once more, she had survived their New Year's Eve party, where her white apartment became even whiter with everyone dressed in the traditional good-luck white, celebrating a mandatory happiness. Her manicurist had polished her nails white.

Maybe next year she wouldn't be there and no one would even notice. Where would she be, next December thirty-first?

The multicolored butterfly beat its weightless wings as it flew so small over a forbidden quarry and softly brushed against a money tree that had never sprouted. That night Maria Inês once more believed it just might be possible.

She tossed a tote bag onto the bed and began to slowly open the drawers in her closet, almost with curiosity, almost as if she was not quite sure what she would find there.

Summer was also the season for mosquitoes. Common house mosquitoes or "tumblers," slow and stupid, easy to kill, and nervous sand flies, tiny and black, that buzzed around their ears. Tomás and Clarice lit an anti-mosquito smoke spiral to chase them off. Tomás still held his empty glass, and Clarice's eyes rested there, on his hands.

The smoke spiral burned very slowly. For the first time, Tomás told Clarice, like someone confessing a foolish act of shoplifting or a laughable secret: I thought about a particular painting the first time I saw your sister.

Clarice looked at him with mild curiosity.

He said a painting by Whistler called *Girl in White* or *Symphony in White No. 1.*

Sacred words. Worthy of an individual sanctuary, erected in praise of a god of which he was the only follower, thought Tomás. That myth died when he stepped beyond the boundaries of his own dreams, which were now as if mummified and cursed, dormant beneath the earth.

They apparently did not even interest Clarice, whose words sounded somewhat trivial: do you have a reproduction of it around here?

He knew the painting by heart. The background was some sort of heavy curtain, white. The fur rug (it looked like a wolf or a bear, the mouth open and the teeth white and the snout raised) under the invisible feet of the girl. A bouquet of white flowers fallen there, on the rug. And the girl with a pensive expression, her face emerging solid from the frame of her dark hair. Pale, her hands almost as white as her long dress. Her lips only slightly colored. A delicate white flower in her left hand.

He hadn't saved any reproductions of the painting, and Clarice went back to trying to extract a sound from the rim of the empty glass (without success: it was not fine crystal, but thick glass, and had once housed seven and a half ounces of jelly).

Clarice and Tomás had met more than twenty years earlier, at Afonso Olímpio's wake, and he had been perplexed to notice, at the time, that neither she nor Maria Inês wept over their father's death.

They actually seemed to be removed, as if they were in a trance. That happened not long before Clarice finally asked Ilton Xavier for a divorce and right before Maria Inês accepted the first formal proposal for marriage made by her second cousin João Miguel Azzopardi. Which, in turn, beat Tomás's proposal to the draw, and the young artist had to bury his passion like a spurned dog buries a bone in the backyard.

Tomás said: I've lost the ability, and Clarice looked at him with curiosity. That flexibility, he continued, that I had when I was with Maria Inês.

He had practiced yoga and had learned to twist himself into admirable positions. He was now a set of rusty gears.

If that is indeed an ability, suggested Clarice. Maybe it's more a question of will, you know, all of that, falling in love, not falling in love. Giving up.

I think will almost always has to yield to ability, Tomás reminded her.

The dog howled softly. Clarice nudged it with her foot to rouse it out of its nightmare and said maybe it's just the opposite.

All afternoon it had been promising rain. They could finally hear the first heavy drops outside.

The Official Versions

Rio de Janeiro was very humid. That was the first thing Clarice noticed about living in the city (in the falsely woven myth of her fantasies).

She commented to her great-aunt Berenice, on their first walk through the streets of Flamengo: sometimes the ocean has a strong smell, doesn't it?

Her great-aunt Berenice smiled, breathed in deeply, and closed her eyes. Yes, isn't it wonderful?

Clarice did not want to disagree with her. I think I'm not used to it yet.

Beneath the lightweight and completely outdated dress she was wearing, she could feel the sweat forming in her armpits, in the curve of her breasts. They walked to the Largo do Machado Square, where her great-aunt Berenice bought corn to feed the pigeons, and then they had ice cream, and on the way back home they had to quicken their pace because, according to Great-Aunt Berenice, a drunken beggar was following them. At the corner of Almirante Tamandaré Street they managed to lose him.

Suddenly Clarice laughed. She found all that to be very amusing, a burst of childhood caught her by surprise. She looked at the tall buildings and she thought they were beautiful, and the people and the cars. She even liked the low constant hum that conducted everything—the opposite of the silence on the farm—and which could, nonetheless, also become silence when she got used to hearing it. Clarice laughed and her great-aunt Berenice, looking at her, also laughed.

Clarice now had a modest studio of sorts for herself. Great-Aunt Berenice separated a small part of her enormous laundry area off the kitchen so that Clarice could make her sculptures there and emptied an entire storage shelf in the unoccupied servant's bedroom so that she would have a place to store them and let them dry.

Sometimes Clarice helped Great-Aunt Berenice in the kitchen, like the afternoon she finally learned the recipe for *casadinhos* sandwich cookies. *3 cups flour. 2 cups sugar. 6 yolks. 3 egg whites. 1 teaspoon baking powder.* She thought about Lina a lot at the beginning and later not so much. *Beat the egg whites until stiff, add the yolks and sugar, beat well, add the flour sifted with the baking powder.*

There were days that the strong sea winds swept through the Flamengo apartment unlike anything Clarice had ever known at the farm. It was not unusual for the windows to become sticky with the salt air. And everything rusted more quickly.

Spoon the mixture onto a greased cookie sheet and bake. When golden, join two cookies together with the filling of your choice (caramelized milk, jelly, etc.). Make a glaze frosting by mixing 8 oz. of powdered sugar with water until it forms a thin cream and dip the double cookies in the glaze. Put aside for the frosting to harden.

In March came the heavy rains that blackened the asphalt streets and caused the pedestrians to hasten their steps. Clarice enjoyed watching the parades of umbrellas passing along the sidewalks on Catete and Laranjeiras Streets, but she found the puddles that formed on the shop floors, building entranceways, and church tiles singularly morose.

On Sundays they went to mass, sometimes to Glória Church, which was closer, and sometimes to Outeiro Church, which was perched up high on a hill overlooking the face of the sea.

Clarice still had the same dreams, at night. She would continue to have them during those long years that passed by very slowly (in the future she would reformulate that idea: *during those long years during which I passed by very slowly—for time stands still, but creatures pass by*). She grew, celebrated birthdays, made friends, a few, not many. And she had a boyfriend in 1966. His name was Almir and no one in her family, except for her Great-Aunt Berenice, ever knew of his existence.

The first year she visited the farm twice and was not surprised to see that no one there talked about Lina anymore. The house was full of people on the occasions of her visits and always insistently frequented by Ilton Xavier.

When he and Clarice met again, in July, he asked: and so, do you remember?

The moon was a sliver now, an exclamation in the sky while they sat on the front porch, drinking hot chocolate, so close to the voices of the adults in the living room.

Ilton Xavier held Clarice's hands and she hissed a reprimand.

Where, then? But at that moment the uncle from Jabuticabais (who had once told a joke that Otacília considered improper) appeared on the porch carrying a telescope and followed by an entourage of children, including Maria Inês. It's a great night for looking at stars, he said. (They set up the telescope on a small mound of earth, a few paces in front of the porch, and Maria Inês was amazed to discover that a single star visible to the naked eye could multiply into dozens of other stars. And to discover that Saturn had real rings.)

Clarice and Ilton Xavier had their correspondence, and their letters made them believe bonds were being formed, gave them a rough impression of intimacy being gently carved out and covered in concrete. The letters created and fed fantasies. There was calligraphy and there were poems, at times copied without due credit, and others, immature and sincere, written in one sitting, and there were drops of perfume and dried flower petals, a photograph, sometimes a magazine clipping.

Dating by correspondence is good, her great-aunt Berenice said once, with a touch of melancholy dripping from her voice. Then she became playful: as a matter of fact dating is *always* good!

Before Clarice knew it, she and Ilton Xavier were boyfriend and girlfriend, officially. And shortly thereafter they were already talking about an engagement, which seemed to be a result of the natural course of things.

In the meantime, between the summers in the company of her cousin João Miguel and those long years that her sister's absence both distressed and reassured her, Maria Inês was growing up.

As did the trees and bushes around her house and the wild woods in places where no one ventured. Only the pasture where the cattle grazed remained low like a close-cropped head of hair. The mango tree where she and João Miguel had played on a swing made from a piece of rope and an old tire reached maturity. Moss began to grow on its branches. A bromeliad settled on the branch of a purple ipê tree and produced a single red blossom. The bougainvilleas near the kitchen door became a knotted confusion of twisted branches and fierce-colored flowers. The snake plants and the split-leaf philodendrons multiplied along the gully that ran by the house and, in the orchard, the black jaboticaba trees cast shadows and the slender papaya trees exploded with fruit. A starfruit tree had shot up before anyone realized it, and now, yellow waxen fruit hung from its branches.

Only the money tree that Maria Inês and João Miguel had planted had never decided to sprout—but the cousins no longer thought about that, of course. They now had other pressing needs.

There were many things João Miguel would never know. But he did notice that Maria Inês was not particularly welcome in her own house, a situation that the years seemed to polish and sharpen, to make more explicit without the least amount of self-consciousness.

She also wanted to get away. It was not so easy, however, to deduce what sort of things Otacília and Afonso Olímpio arbitrated. In fact, Maria Inês exasperated them both, her false subordination exasperated them, her fake concern. Cards hidden up her sleeves. Maria Inês was always putting her nose where she shouldn't, saying things she had been taught not to say (like the time the priest from Jabuticabais came to give his annual blessing of the farm and she asked, after kissing his thin, cold hand: have you never been with a woman, a real woman, ever?), showing up at the wrong times and hearing too much, reading on the sly. She liked to gallop (she fell off horses three different times, once breaking an arm) and swam in the river in the cold rain, in the late afternoon, when the sky was unsettled. She like to pick up toads and beetles in her hands.

Maria Inês still liked to go up to the forbidden quarry. Alone, most of the time. In the summer, with João Miguel.

Look at the Ipês Farm, she pointed.

There you go again with that story.

She then stopped, but the dead woman's cries seemed to echo in her ears, the husband's shining eyes (two marbles) and foaming mouth were mirrored in her imagination. And now there was also the terrified image of the lover, his impotent nudity, the limp, pathetic penis between his legs, his slacks and shoes tossed on the bedroom floor, and his hands still hot with her smell. The cold sweat on his brow.

João Miguel and Maria Inês began to have something else in common besides their double names. As if they could foresee the future, a sort of complicity, even if the prophesized future and the real future clashed a little.

Everything had to follow a course, nonetheless, and Maria Inês grew up without asking permission. By the age of fifteen, she was already the distinct promise of a woman.

They received the news of João Miguel's mother on a cold evening, the kind of evening that is inflated with expectations and guards secrets under its tongue. Or coins on its eyes, for the boatman. A night similar to a rite of passage. Someone showed up on horseback to break the news. And then everything remained the same and the only comment Maria Inês heard her mother make was poor thing, now she'll be at peace. And Afonso Olímpio said Clarice can go to the funeral and represent the family.

Maria Inês went outside. She was alone—normally João Miguel would have spent his July vacation there, but that year something had kept him in Rio de Janeiro. Perhaps some sort of vague premonition.

Inside the house, the grandfather clock sounded a discreet polyrhythm with the rusty back and forth of the rocking chair where Afonso Olímpio read a leather-bound book with gold letters on the spine that said *Amadis of Gaul. Adapted by Afonso Lopes Vieira*. In the same room, neither very close to nor very far from her husband, Otacília embroidered an outfit for her cousin's baby, which was due soon. Outside the world whispered, and it had many, many voices.

Maria Inês made a fire with some logs, out of sight from the others. Then she got several old sheets of newspaper and began to form them into balloon-like so-called *galinhas pretas—black hens*, for the shape they took—and burn them, and they rose black and swollen and glowing against the night and fell farther off, enlivened by the wind. One of those *galinhas pretas* was blown even farther away and fell next to the bamboo grove, at the exact point where the pasture on the side of the house began. The fire started slowly, but everything was favorable, the wind, the drought, and in the blink of an eye there were merry orange flames taking over the bamboo, which crackled and hypnotized Maria Inês. She stayed sitting where she was, watching.

When Afonso Olímpio and Otacília were awakened from their pastimes, which drew them in and pretended to comfort them, a particularly tall bamboo had already fallen onto the pasture, in flames.

They were only able to control the fire in the early morning—ten men working non-stop—and the only thing left of the pasture was a long black strip that would take a long time to recuperate.

It was probably that morning that Otacília turned to her husband and said, always looking away from him: you know it's on purpose. Those things she does. But Afonso Olímpio did not respond. Otacília said it's time to send her away.

Things remained on hold for a short while. They held their breath and sunk into sleep. The months that followed that winter were longer and much sadder. João Miguel began to join his father on his trips because that was part of the training reserved for him, which he accepted without much protest. Of course, there was a lawyer in his future, a lawyer with a white apartment in Upper Leblon, who liked to go to Venice and play tennis for reasons beyond the more obvious ones.

Six months. A year. And surrounding Maria Inês was a slimy solitude that took her breath away.

When Maria Inês and her second cousin next met he was growing a ridiculous moustache that happily did not last long. And he seemed much older.

It was in the Jabuticabais church, while Ilton Xavier, in a beautiful dark suit with a white carnation in his lapel, a pearl in the knot (very well tied) of his gray tie, waited trembling like a leaf at the altar for Clarice, his bride.

Maria Inês asked João Miguel how are things going.

Okay. I'm studying a lot.

She knew why he was studying so much, knew it was in preparation for the entrance exams to law school. He had on a suit and he wore it with more ease than Maria Inês would have imagined. She wore a horrendous dress, avocado green, which ended abruptly and unsubtly at her knees, with full sleeves, unflattering to her shoulders.

It was cold on that late afternoon, even though it was already October. The interior walls of the small Jabuticabais church were blue with spiral scrolls that had one day been gold. There was a visible leak in one corner, which had turned a small section of the ceiling black with mold. The stained-glass windows were unpretentious, simple mosaics that revealed a dove here, a radiant sun there, a cross. On the opposite side the designs were repeated in different colors.

All the long pews of well-worn dark wood were decorated with white daisies and an occasional lily. On the altar there was a large arrangement of yellow and white flowers. The women present were almost all exaggeratedly overdressed.

Clarice was exaggeratedly overdressed. Her wedding dress looked like Carnival, a joke, a gag. But she was very serious inside her smile, under her lipstick, blush, and blue eye shadow, beneath her cloth-flowered wreath, in the ruby choker that belonged to Ilton Xavier's family and in her lace dress, in her high heels that killed her feet.

She took part in the ceremony as if it were someone else's wedding. She calmly received the wedding band from Ilton Xavier's nervous hands and tried to remember, step by step, how she had ended up there. She couldn't. Her parents and mother- and father-in-law and bridesmaids and groomsmen were all in her peripheral vision, merry splotches of red, blue, yellow, and black. She distracted herself by paying attention to them as she locked her eyes on the priest without seeing him. She did not hear one word of the sermon. But she did hear the organist and violinist play some Bach—off key, it was true, but what difference did it make? Afterwards one of Ilton Xavier's aunts, with her red hair pulled back in a twist and heavy earrings stretching her earlobes, sang Gounod's *Ave Maria*.

That made Clarice happy. And she was still happy when the priest gave Ilton Xavier permission to kiss the bride (although he could have dispensed with that permission), and she imagined that yes, maybe now everything would be different. She closed her eyes for the kiss the way she had seen girls do in films. But the instant she felt the contact of the relatively familiar lips of Ilton Xavier on hers, she half opened her eyes. First she saw the stained-glass windows of the small church, then she noticed it was overflowing with people, then she looked at Otacília and Alfonso Olímpio and found them to be unusually large. She closed her eyes again, this time tightly.

When you are afraid, what is the wisest attitude to have? The most convenient? The most efficient? Close your eyes or open them? Give up, lose control, turn your back? Run? Or face it, grab hold, examine, control?

Clarice stepped down from the altar and followed the worn-out red carpet. The people were stacked on either side, wherever she looked, she felt like the prow of a boat parting the waters.

Clarice was passing through the church the way a knife slices through a stick of butter. She was cutting her life in half, deliberately. She wanted to recognize herself in the division: before and after. And her pagan Christ was there at her side, he, Ilton Xavier, the savior. Who loved her because she had no secrets.

That night, after the reception, Otacília and Maria Inês found themselves in the kitchen. It was no surprise when the mother said to the daughter, so now the time has come to talk about you.

Talk about Maria Inês. As if it were possible to talk about Maria Inês.

She said I want to go study in Rio de Janeiro, too. Do you think Great-Aunt Berenice will let me live there, now that Clarice has left?

(Great-Aunt Berenice had gone to the wedding, of course. With her big-city clothes and habits. With her old-maid idiosyncrasies. With her allergy to insect bites. She had brought in her suitcase a sophisticated present that she had hoped would be unforgettable: she imagined Clarice and her husband, decades later, showing the Christofle silver to their grandchildren and saying this was a present from the dearly deceased Great-Aunt Berenice.)

Otacília spoke without looking at Maria Inês while she served herself a glass of water from the clay water filter (they didn't need a filter, because the tap water came directly from the underground spring. It was merely an excess of zeal applied to the wrong situation, with an erroneous objective, with results that were dispensable, superfluous).

I believe Aunt Berenice will have you, said Otacília.

Maria Inês suggested maybe I could go in November.

Otacília shook her head and said December is better.

She did not explain why. Maria Inês did not want to ask. She didn't like to give anyone the upper hand, to ask questions, to make requests. Otacília waited for Maria Inês to ask why December, but the question never came. For an instant the mother and the daughter stood looking at each other, between the refrigerator and the kitchen sink, and bore an elastic arch of tension like a bout of arm wrestling.

December, then, Maria Inês confirmed, and her voice had the tone of a formal agreement. It smelled of a lawyer's office, with stamps and notary publics. Then she almost wanted to ask about Otacília's health, but she merely watched her mother walk away, small, weak, sickly, benumbed, useless. The real Otacília would now have to face the loneliness of Afonso Olímpio's company. The husband whom she had chosen at the age of twenty-eight, on the happiest and most unreal day of her life.

A few minutes later João Miguel came in, without his coat, without his tie, with the first two buttons of his shirt unbuttoned.

And so?

It was a question that was not asking anything. Maria Inês chewed on her fingernails and watched a small lizard that drew an uneven trail on the ceiling.

Your mother doesn't seem well to me. She should go see a doctor in Rio, João Miguel said, genuinely concerned.

And Maria Inês agreed with callous disinterest.

Then she picked up a three-legged stool and went into the pantry and brought back a half-empty bottle of liqueur.

She commented, victorious, they think I don't know where they hide this.

She filled a cup. Homemade orange liqueur.

Do you want some?

João Miguel said no, that he had drunk enough at the reception. No one controlled how much he drank. He was almost a grown man.

After emptying her cup of liqueur, Maria Inês said I'm going in December.

To Rio?

Yes, to Rio.

But that's soon! This is great!

João Miguel began to talk about the places they would go, the films they would see, the beaches they would frequent, the clubs where they would go to dance, and the ice cream shops where they would try pistachio or hazelnut ice cream (big-city treats).

Of course Tomás was not in his plans. Nor were several other things that would happen in Maria Inês's life, and in his own life, and in their life together that they would start in a few years as man and wife. Furtive realities, at times as cheerful as the banners for the Saint John festivities in June, at times as woeful as a bird in the rain, realities that for a while caressed and then trampled, that did harm, that corroded like rust. And that sat there silent like a sleepy, gloomy angel.

Clarice's marriage lasted six sluggish years. However, on that October evening, her wedding night, she was trembling with the perspective in which she still believed. She dabbed on some perfume and put on a salmon-rose nightgown trimmed in guipure lace. And she studied her fingernails, amused to see them polished the color of wine and as long as a movie star's nails. When Ilton Xavier came around, however, and lay down at her side and slowly began to take possession of the territory that had been granted his property by the state and by the Holy Mother Roman Catholic and Apostolic Church, Clarice knew that there was some sort of sentence that hung over her. It felt something like an incurable disease, definitive, irreversible.

After Ilton Xavier (the gentle, in-love Ilton Xavier) finished his not very ambitious performance and curled up in sleep like a child, in the fetal position, hugging his pillow, she pulled the sheet and the blanket up and covered him to his shoulders.

It was a cold night and Ilton Xavier closed his eyes and pretended to sleep, but he was thinking over a question that he did not have the courage to ask—could there have been *another* man in her life? He himself was not very experienced. But he had learned, through books and men's conversations, what it was supposed to be like for a woman the first time. It had not exactly been like that with Clarice. But he ended up deciding to forget about the subject. It was the only possible choice for Ilton Xavier, *to forget about the subject* and to live happy-with-his-adored-wife. He forgot about the subject and was happy-with-his-adored-wife until the day she left him without any previous warning.

Clarice put her wedding night lingerie back on, and then a navy blue sweater. She slipped on her funny wool slipper socks, handwoven, and left the bedroom.

The house of Ilton Xavier's parents was not anything like her parents' house. It was, for starters, much older, over a century old.

Slaves had erected the walls with money from growing coffee. A baron had left his determined footsteps on the wooden floors and his face in some of the yellowed portraits in oval frames. Francisco Miranda, 1875, Clarice read on one of the portraits. It was also much larger, the house, with ten bedrooms and not just four. It had a small chapel with images of the Virgin Mary with Christ in her lap, of Saint Joseph and of Saint Jude Thaddeus, and a prayer desk upholstered in antique-green velvet. There were multiple rooms where Clarice thought she could get lost. In one of them, which was called the Reading Room (they all had names: Reading Room, Music Room, Breakfast Room, Games Room, Dining Room, Sitting Room), there was a stuffed hawk and a stuffed baby alligator that she would have loved to throw out or at least hide on a tall shelf in the closet. There were trophies and medals. And there were so many faces in old photographs that she thought that even living there she would never be capable of associating them with the right names.

She cracked open the tall window in the Reading Room and the room was cut by the milky spirit of the moonlight. The small pendulum clock showed three ten. The night hour that is almost always lost in sleep. Then she leaned on the windowsill and saw that the valley was soaked with the pleasant light of the huge full moon, yellow as butter. The river ran by at a short distance. She couldn't see it, but she could make out the distinct murmur of its current. Beyond the river was a vast pasture, then the road and then the hill that looked alive in the moonlight, an animal lurking, and beyond the hill, her parents' house.

One could get away, but not that far.

Clarice wandered through the other rooms and then went to the kitchen to peek at the cats. There were lots of them, all curled together at the foot of the wood-burning stove that still emitted some heat—like the body of a lover well into the night.

Like Ilton Xavier's body innocently happy in his state of inertia. She went back to the bedroom, inaudible in her slipper socks.

Ilton Xavier had turned in the bed and uncovered half of his body: his left leg, his genitals, and stomach were exposed without shame. Clarice once more straightened the sheets and covered her husband to his shoulders. She then noticed that even in the darkness his hair was surprisingly blonde, an inheritance from his European ancestry (the Swiss colony in Nova Friburgo). Ilton Xavier had learned to speak German at home and had taught Clarice the numbers from one to ten and a noun or two: *die Blume. Die Schwarzkirsche* for jabuticaba, the black cherry. *Der Wald. Der Stern. Die Liebe.*

Die Liebe. Love. Clarice lay down on the bed, on top of the covers, without removing her slipper socks and her sweater. From behind her closed eyelids, she waited for the first ray of sunlight and for the first rooster to come and crow beneath her window.

Symphony in White

At that time the Flamengo apartment was a very attractive chaos. The smell of paint overpowered even Tomás's occasional endeavors at frying, on the days he attempted, almost always without success, to test his talents as a cook. Most of the time he ate out, a sandwich, a special in some cheap diner. He was always broke, of course.

The sky was cloudy on the morning Tomás woke up and realized he was twenty years old. His perspectives were as grandiose as they were unorganized, and he had not yet realized he needed to tame and civilize his own talent. Render it capable of becoming an accomplishment, a recognizable mark in the world, not just dreams and musings.

Clad in a worn-out dress shirt that was his work uniform, threadbare at the collar and wretchedly stained all over, he regarded his paintings, his sketches, his studies, his drawings, his materials. He thought about James Abbott McNeill Whistler and about one of his paintings, done in 1862, of a girl with pale features, in front of a pale background, wearing a pale dress, who had now reincarnated in a young girl leaning on the balcony of a neighboring apartment. Impossible to dissociate art from passion, Tomás had sketchbooks of furious drawings.

And she, the girl in white, was listening to ballet music.

Tchaikovsky, maybe, he thought. Through his window the fortissimos reached Tomás. The girl's thick, wild hair hung heavy, but her body swayed gently from one side to the other.

Tomás saw the girl, but she did not see him. Without a hint of self-consciousness, she left the balcony and returned to the darkness of her bedroom, leaned over in front of the dressing table and half-comically studied her own face in the oval mirror. Then she picked up the edges of her white dress that had belonged to her older sister and became a ballerina, making movements (slightly languid) with her arms and legs. Tomás watched—not because the girl was particularly beautiful, but because she *was* that Whistler painting.

And now she was on her way, that morning so pathetically real. Maria Inês, the faded spot left by a painting that had been removed after years of life on the same wall. Tomás's life that had ended before it began.

When he was twenty years old, Tomás was obsessed with drawing her, the neighbor who liked to practice ballet steps in front of her mirror, backed by her long, thick, dark hair. Sketch her, capture her, keep her, love her. He pulled out his best paper, his best pencils and charcoal sticks and pastel chalks and embarked on that risky enterprise: to know Maria Inês. Which was destined to never end.

Maria Inês was seventeen years old. She received Clarice's letters from the backlands of the state: it's strange that we've simply switched places. You in the big city, in the room I myself occupied at our great-aunt's house, and I back here, with the same hills, the same faces. In fact, I think that it's more fitting this way.

The two sisters didn't exchange that many letters, and they were insufficient in form and frequency. From Rio de Janeiro, the big city (where there were airports and planes flew at low altitudes), Maria Inês wrote that she was doing well in her studies, high school, piano, and French classes. Which was not entirely true. And she wrote that she enjoyed living in that roomy apartment near the ocean. She liked the big mirror above the dressing table in her bedroom.

From the farm Clarice wrote that she was doing well in her marriage and that she enjoyed living with Ilton Xavier and his parents in that century-old plantation house with sparkling white walls and blue windows. Which was not entirely false. She had half a bed all to herself and an armoire and also a dressing table. The land of Ilton Xavier's parents neighbored on Otacília and Afonso Olímpio's land.

One could get away, but not that far.

Maria Inês was finishing high school and also taking piano lessons for no particular reason. She hated scales and arpeggios. At least three times a week her second cousin João Miguel paid her and her great aunt a visit. He sometimes brought flowers or chocolate.

He's very interested in you, Great-Aunt Berenice would say with her warm voice, a voice acquired from decades of conversations with dogs, cats, canaries, and other pets.

Maria Inês knew that. I guess you're right, I guess he *is* very interested in me.

I think he's going to end up asking you to marry him, commented Great-Aunt Berenice.

And Maria Inês just smiled.

But it did not take her long to notice, however, that a certain neighbor in the building across the street spent a lot of time looking out his window, often with a notebook in hand, apparently drawing.

Was he looking at her? It could be that he was reproducing her building, the windows, the façade. They said it was a good example of Art Deco architecture (the first time she had heard of the term Maria Inês had pronounced it *ar-tee-DEH-co,* until they corrected her, that's French, honey, *ahr-deh-CO!*). *Art Déco.* She lived with her great-aunt Berenice in an Art Deco building that had been built in the twenties.

Maybe the boy in the other building was studying architecture. She speculated, until the day he decided to wave, and Maria Inês waved back. He shouted, hi there, girl from the fifth floor, and she answered, amused, somewhat childlike, hi there, guy from the . . . sixth floor?

He motioned. I did some sketches. Do you want to see?

Maria Inês thought for a moment and then finally asked—as if the answer would furnish her with some sort of certificate of good conduct: what's your name?

Tomás, he answered, and she nodded.

We can meet at the entrance.

My building?

No. Mine.

It was already clear, from the very first moment, that she would be calling the shots.

In the entrance hall of the Art Deco building there were two mirrors that faced one another and attempted to reproduce infinity, and there were two identical benches. Maria Inês chose one and sat down and saw Tomás drawing near. She noticed his eyes long before she saw that the edges of his fingernails were dirty with paint. It was Maria Inês in the sketches. Dressed in white in most of them.

Will you give me one of these?

Whichever one you want.

And she burst out okay, thanks, drop by sometime and meet my great-aunt, it's been a pleasure, see you around.

She waved her hands about as she moved in the direction of the elevators. Tomás could still see her for an instant caught between the two mirrors.

His sketch won a space on Maria Inês's bedroom wall, above her headboard. Great-Aunt Berenice, her clothes covered in cat hair, went close to snoop, and let out a deep sigh. How pitiful, she thought, that the body is so out of step with the mind. She felt old. It seemed there were no more words she needed to understand. There was no one to ask her questions, her world was quiet. When she started to become melodramatic like that, Great-Aunt Berenice ran the risk of feeling even older and falling into a vicious circle, but she possessed an unusual ability to turn her back on certain thoughts. She went over to the window and saw the young man on the sixth floor of the building across the street. He looked handsome, but at that age they all looked handsome. Dark curly hair. She waved with a great-aunt's lack of shyness, and her heavy bracelets rattled on her pudgy wrist. Her flesh shook beneath her caramel-colored blouse.

Tomás remembered perfectly Great-Aunt Berenice's smile in bas-relief and the dimples in her cheeks.

Time stands still, but creatures pass by.

And those bracelets full of charms. And the baby-like indentations in her elbows. He remembered the excitement twinkling in her eyes when he was finally received at her apartment. And the avid and gentle manner in which she pretended to *not suspect anything*.

Tomás and Maria Inês began to meet in the afternoon to get away from everyone else. As if they were animals setting out on a migration

for two. They strolled along the Flamengo shore, spoke in code, and laughed at people passing by.

Squanderers, young, they were in a hurry, but they wasted time. Reality took on special configurations to which only they held the keys.

On a certain afternoon, their lips met, eager and without surprise. So in that the young artist beat the cousin João Miguel to the draw, who nonetheless had been a part of Maria Inês's life long before (and who would continue to visit her regularly, always in the evening, well-groomed and sweet-smelling, with roses and chocolate).

At Tomás's apartment, there was, besides the smell of paint, an out-of-tune upright piano with the middle D-note silent. That afternoon, when he went to the kitchen to make some coffee, Maria Inês sat in front of the keyboard and lightly ran her fingers across the white keys. Then she began to play the simple pieces she had learned in her handful of piano lessons. Tomás came back from the kitchen and was about to confess that he had run out of coffee, but she was playing, and so he sat cross-legged on the wooden floor to listen to whatever it was, anything. Anything, bad or good, played well or poorly, as long as it was her, her body, her fingers. Maria Inês's music, small beginning pieces.

It would be possible, it would have to be possible. What ran through Maria Inês's heart would remain opaque and secret, but an embrace was formed in the arc of Tomás's desire. Her back and her curved arms, her body swaying as she played and her head to the right and to the left accompanying her hands.

She would later say please, Tomás, don't fall in love with me, and he would ask, smiling, why not? to which she would respond because I'm not in love with you. At that moment, however, and even after her revelation of not being in love, Tomás reassured himself: it would be possible. It would have to be possible. Because his love would perhaps be sufficient for them both, like a generous serving in a restaurant. Enough to feed two people, a double portion of desire capable of bearing the weight of both destinies, and of even joining them together.

To imagine, from that moment on, a life without Maria Inês would be the same as living it inside-out. As *dis*living. It was at that exact moment while she sat at the piano that love struck, and from then on it made no difference to Tomás what she might say or how she might act. Because at times love feeds on its own improbability. Because at times the other person causes a dizziness that is too broad, too encompassing, and the only way to embrace it and try and organize it is through the boundlessness of love—just as a drunk has that first shot in the morning to cure a hangover from the previous night.

Tomás closed the curtains as a polite precaution. Everything was effortless, the mildness of the fall afternoon, the humid presence of the sea, their murmurs. There was the overwhelming impression that, after all, it had always been that way between them. He was thin, quite thin, but Maria Inês felt comfortable running her fingers along his shoulder blades as she had done on the torso of an unfinished sketch, and she wasn't surprised. Thunder was rolling across the sky—it was going to rain.

Then he said I'd already been thinking about this for a long time. And everything fell into place, and he smiled and thought he saw mirrored in her his own smile.

She was up before seven o'clock, which was not that unusual. What was surprising was that her daughter was already awake, and more than that, bathed, a light cotton dress covering her light body, leather sandals instead of her eternally bare feet. A thin silver ring on her toe, on closer look. The aroma of baby cologne.

The white apartment was going into hibernation. There were no servants sweeping through its arteries in search of dirty glasses or spider webs, smoothing out bedspreads, putting place mats on the dining room table, picking popcorn up off the floor in front of the television. The appliances were all mute, with the exception of the coffee maker that discreetly let off steam in the kitchen. There was no João Miguel, who was probably asleep in his seat, thirty thousand feet in the air.

Eduarda had a small Peruvian backpack decorated with embroidered figures, tiny men and women in hats, animals that must be llamas. A *recuerdo*, a souvenir from a trip to Machu Picchu. Maria Inês had a tote bag that duplicated the same initials on her key case. All together, their baggage possessed a healthy minimalism—of course, there would be no need for excesses. It was better to subtract, remove, like a sculptor in the face of a block of stone. It was better to be less, to become smaller, to be empty-handed.

For no special reason, they went along the beach. It was the longest route, but also the prettiest. The seaside sidewalk was full of pilgrims going nowhere, who came and went, in a hurry and sweating and multicolored in their gym clothes and expensive sneakers. Bicycles zoomed by on the bicycle path, and some skates, as well. Nannies in white uniforms pushed the pink offspring of their employers, who would be at the office in smart suits and high heels.

They came and went, they went, they came back. The tourists were recognizable at a good distance, for always being taller and much redder, at times with odd, very blond eyebrows. The prostitutes were identifiable by their short, tight skirts, their stiletto heels, and their evening-before faces, still sipping a beer with the last client in the shade of a food stand. For them, the night was not yet over, which was a somewhat brutal anachronism.

When their car stopped at a red light, a young girl came up asking for money, she hit the closed window with her open hand and Maria Inês shook her head. The girl remained there, empty-eyed, and Maria Inês noticed a group of people sitting on the edge of the sidewalk: a mother, two children, and a baby lying down who played with a paper bag. They were all uniformly dusky and the mother looked young. Then Maria Inês noticed the baby more closely—five, six months old, maybe less. It was lying on top of a piece of newspaper and turned from one side, to the other. The baby's two legs were missing and it had on diapers that didn't fit properly because diapers were not designed for babies with no legs. In the place of the right leg a stump moved softly, on the other side there was not even that.

Is that your brother over there?

Yes.

He doesn't have any legs?

No, and on one hand he has five fingers and on the other one he only has three.

The baby played with a paper bag as it lay on top of a piece of newspaper on the avenue sidewalk.

The girl explained my mother went to pee one day and my brother popped out, he was born early. That's why he's got those defects.

Bicycles zoomed along the bike path. The light turned green and in the rearview mirror Maria Inês could see a black Grand Cherokee deftly zigzagging in an attempt to run over a careless pigeon that had decided to land on the street, but the pigeon managed to escape.

The girl begged lady, give me some money. Her tangled hair held back with red barrettes. Then she said lady, buy some chewing gum.

The pigeon that had escaped the Grand Cherokee's attack landed on a windowsill where a cleaning woman had two-thirds of her body hanging out while she cleaned the glass windows. And then the cars began to honk because everyone was late for work or because they were hysterical and couldn't help but honk. No one looked at the baby any longer. And the traffic lights changed, and the cars went by, one after another.

Maria Inês and Eduarda reached the Rio-Niterói Bridge where the traffic was slightly congested near the tollbooths. Eduarda curled up like a fetus, turned sideways in her seat with her back to Maria Inês.

As the car proceeded and the first hour of the trip slipped by, a parade of pastures began out the window and not particularly beautiful cattle. Every once in a while, a precariously constructed stand on the highway's edge, where turnovers, sugarcane juice, bread, and sausage were sold. Dried bananas. When they passed near some small town, the car shook over speed bumps that were always multiplying because the towns were growing, and they grew along the highways—then they would move the highway and new towns would grow around the new highway, and in a few years speed bumps were there again. Pachydermous trucks rolled along piled with crates of bananas, sacks of cement, or cages carrying live chickens.

Eduarda appeared to be asleep, her body shook in rhythm with the road. Maria Inês was listening to music. João Miguel was flying over the ocean and dreaming, Maria Inês knew what his dream was about and she could almost see it, as if she were seeing a film at the movie theater. It was about Venice.

And (Maria Inês could now bring things together) she also thought about Clarice and about Tomás. She no longer knew them, and this was like not recognizing a part of herself.

But now she was fitting the pieces into a mosaic. There was a specific place for Venice and for a young man named Paolo. For a tennis instructor and an ex-wife (Luciana) of a cousin who worked in the film industry. For João Miguel. For the *vecchio* Azzopardi. For his bottles of Chianti, for a baritone named Bernardo Águas, for a daughter, for twin Olfa knife scars, and a C-section. She needed to organize it all and find an appropriate place for each thing. A place for that damned multicolored butterfly.

The minutes, the hours, the days, and the years (of youth, of yoga) that Tomás spent at Maria Inês's side smelled like vanilla or jasmine or calla lilies, anything white and lovely. At that time he still did not *know*. He was like an Adam before the apple—before the truth.

Or: a set of truths. Made of the same substance that lined the walls of that Ipês Farm, which Maria Inês had told him about on one of their first outings. Can you imagine? Do you think he loved the woman? Do you think he was crazy?

Tomás was trying to grab hold of Maria Inês's hands and found the story about the Ipês Farm to be very inappropriate. But she went back to the same story, months later, as he drew an arabesque with India ink on her bare buttocks. (Do you think that when they set him on fire he was already dead? Or maybe he was only *half* dead? Burning to death must be the worst death. Worse than drowning or getting shot or in a car accident. Worse than starving or freezing or . . .)

Just forget about it, Maria Inês.

I can't just forget about it.

And she pulled a pillow towards herself—they were in his parents' bed, which was once more in use and almost seemed happy about it, perfumed and alive again.

There's a huge quarry on that farm, she continued. Up on the hill that's back behind my parents' house. My father forbade us to go up there because from the other side it would be really easy to fall. Even though to this day no one's ever fallen. The quarry ends abruptly, as if you climbed a ladder and all of a sudden the rungs ran out. It's very high. From up there you can see the Ipês Farm.

Someone must live there now.

Maria Inês shook her head while she chewed on the corner of the pillow. And she said their daughter inherited the land, but she abandoned it all and disappeared. Her name was Lindaflor. Poor thing.

The corner of the pillow was damp with her saliva. Tomás began to tell her that he had talked to his parents on the phone the previous night, that they were fine, and he had told them about her, and they had told him it was snowing in Santiago de Chile.

I would love to see snow, he said, childlike, and Maria Inês suggested, why don't you go visit them? which made Tomás sad. Twenty is also an age in which the true dimension of things is turned upside down. In which everything looks like reflections in amusement park mirrors.

Maria Inês, however, had not yet put the forbidden quarry to rest. On the Ipês Farm, the roof tiles blackened with time, the farm was like the carcass of a dead animal, and there inside, beneath the tiles, among the streaked and peeling walls, ghosts howled. There seemed to be some idea there, in that silent womb, in the company of the memory of one crime followed by the other.

And while her body communicated with Tomás's body, a much more profound and abysmal Maria Inês continued to bleed. But she smiled as he enclosed her back in an embrace. He noticed that the nape of her neck was slightly damp with sweat—there in that sacred place where minute curls grew like the sprouts of a plant.

Florian

The days of happiness that Maria Inês and Tomás shared together lasted for a good while, but all the unhappiness was already there, prowling like the spaces between the words of a text. Like a tiger on the dangerous borders of dreams.

She skipped countless French and piano lessons to meet Tomás at his apartment or to wander with him throughout the city, holding hands, finding true redemption in the asphalt and cobblestones that grew from the ground and smothered the earth and vegetation, which had basically been all that she had known until then. The asphalt was firm beneath her feet, and besides, it didn't dirty her shoes.

Tomás was not totally clandestine, he often showed up for proper Sunday afternoon visits at Great-Aunt Berenice's home. Afterwards he would say to Maria Inês, when they were alone: sometimes I think your great-aunt knows what's going on between us, she's got it all figured out and just pretends to be in the dark, but sometimes I think she's just simply naïve.

And Maria Inês shook her head, saying with her gesture: neither one, nor the other.

She and her great-aunt Berenice did not talk very much. Maria Inês was not the kind to open up and she did not like to ask anyone for advice. And she liked having sex without anyone knowing, against all the moral standards her upbringing had imposed on her, against all the moral standards other girls, even in Rio, obeyed at that time.

At times Tomás. At times, João Miguel. The nature of her relationship with her second cousin was distinct, but it perhaps ran deeper, which was not quite a contradiction. Flowers and chocolate and without secret encounters. João Miguel's large body gave the impression that it was too big for him, as if it were loose, a shirt the next size up. With his soul adrift inside, strong-weak, weak-strong. For that reason, he would never be able to know.

In the same way that, years earlier, in that same city, housed in that same room, Clarice had initiated her personal endeavor, so did Maria Inês now begin to put into effect her own project: build a solid life built upon a solid, touchable, visible, nameable base. She needed to proceed carefully, step by step, sufficiently close to and distant from herself.

The first thing she decided was to enter the School of Medicine, even though she was aware that she would never be anything other than a mediocre physician, because she wasn't interested in medicine. But she needed the solid realm of that profession. That would be safer than trying to discover who Maria Inês might, in reality, truly be.

Shortly before Easter vacation, Maria Inês caught a convenient cold that gave her an excuse for not going to the farm. The cold quickly disappeared and Friday night João Miguel showed up for a visit with a bouquet of wild flowers. Great-Aunt Berenice offered him a liqueur that was ruby red, and on Holy Saturday she offered the same liqueur to Tomás, as well as some vanilla wafers that she had just baked and were still warm.

Maria Inês ate the cookies dipping them one by one in her coffee. She had always drunk coffee on the farm since she was small, and it was the medicine that the cook prescribed for headaches, cramps, and other ailments. After the cookies, the coffee, and the liqueur that left her pleasantly mellow, Maria Inês stood up and said, well, Tomás and I are going to meet some friends at the movies now.

He was used to her improvised lies, so he didn't even raise his eyes from the flawless crystal glass he was examining, where a reddish circle rested at the bottom.

Great-Aunt Berenice smiled and two dimples appeared in her cheeks. Her right hand was petting an old Siamese cat and almost looked as if it were separate from her body, escaping, white, from the ruffled cuffs of her turquoise blouse. She didn't want to allow her mind to speculate too much and for that reason she had developed the habit of believing everything that she was officially told. She was capable, for example, of reading the newspaper and believing every single word. In compliance with that principle, she smiled her chubby smile at Maria Inês, accompanied them to the front door and blew them a kiss while they waited for the elevator. She then closed the heavy wood door with slightly creaky hinges and leaned back against it and began to think something but was distracted by a pair of sparrows that landed at her window. She walked toward them slowly, as slow as she possibly could, and minimized the sound her quilted slip-ons made against the floor. But the sparrows sensed her movement and flew away. And Great-Aunt Berenice stopped right there, in the middle of the living room, feeling somewhat empty.

She was Otacília's mother's youngest sister, and the only one who lived in Rio de Janeiro. She had been born in the last year of the nineteenth century, which made her feel like an anachronism, as if she weren't really a part of the times. It was unpleasant, for example, to fill out documents and where it asked for date of birth to have to come face to face with the nineteenth century in front of fresh, rosy-cheeked civil servants who looked as if they had come straight from kindergarten.

Great-Aunt Berenice had been in love in the twenties with a musician, a pianist, who had been friends with composer Heitor Villa-Lobos and writer Mário de Andrade. And who had taken part in the 1922 Week of Modern Art in São Paulo. In Rio, he taught at the National Conservatory of Music and performed beautiful Beethoven and Schubert recitals. And Villa-Lobos, naturally—a composer that Great-Aunt Berenice did not admire, as she liked nothing that the modernists had done, but was embarrassed to admit it. She fell in love with the pianist in spite of his stylistic leanings and perhaps because he still had Beethoven and Schubert to redeem him.

His name was Juan Carlos and he was an Argentinean who had settled in Brazil, two years older than Berenice and splendidly tall. She liked to rest her head on Juan Carlos's shoulder, which appeared to have been made exclusively for that purpose, a shoulder so leanable, with just the right height and muscles.

They dated properly for two and a half years and then became engaged. Berenice began to exhibit on her left ring finger a gem made of gold, diamonds, and an exquisite pearl, while she delighted in Beethoven and Schubert and tolerated Villa-Lobos. In December of the following year, when she had just finished knitting him a white sweater, Juan Carlos had to go to Buenos Aires. To take care of some personal matters. He thought he would be gone a month, maybe two.

He was gone for thirty years and left Berenice with the engagement ring on her finger and a hollow burning in her throat. She always thought that Juan Carlos was about to arrive, and thus irremediably left behind the proper age for marrying, and in 1956, when she ran into him in downtown Rio, he was merely a tall, grey-haired tourist, accompanied by his beautiful Argentinean daughter who did not even speak Portuguese. Berenice had already become a great-aunt.

In the elevator Maria Inês and Tomás kissed like experienced lovers.

Why did you make up that story about the movies?

I don't know, just to get away a little.

When they reached the ground floor and the metal gate opened, Maria Inês said: maybe we really can go to the movies, what do you say?

Clarice's letter arrived ten days later. She had written on a sheet of stationery embossed with her name and a matching envelope, very sophisticated, a present from Ilton Xavier—who loved her because she had no secrets. The letter was formal and well-structured like the others, with topics divided into paragraphs and superficial news about all of them. It grazed lightly on subjects of planting and harvest, heads of cattle, gallons of milk, but changed subjects well before it became boring like some kind of technical report, and talked about the weather, the rain, a certain cousin who had given birth to triplets, a new dress, some sculptures. It was only in the paragraph dedicated to Otacília that Clarice broke her lullaby rhythm and went into more detail, because the illness was no longer a secret, an illness the doctors couldn't name and were treating as if groping in the dark. Otacília was not in good spirits. She complained of aches in her joints, was very tired, continued to lose weight, and sometimes ran a low fever, but she wasn't willing to consult a doctor in Rio de Janeiro, she would stick with the old family doctors who lived in Jabuticabais or in the vicinity and who practiced the type of medicine based on vitamins, tonics, and instructions for almost complete bed rest.

Maria Inês would never become a good physician. But she would have enough curiosity to discover, when it no longer mattered, it was lupus that had tortured Otacília for more than ten years before it killed her.

Clarice's letter ended with best regards and suggested that a visit from Maria Inês would be welcome. That was the prelude. It would not be much longer now.

It would not be much longer now. Two and a half, three hours on the road. Eduarda had woken up.

Mom, do you think we could stop for a minute?

On the way up the mountains there's that diner.

A Parada Predileta—"The Favorite Stopping Place."

Maria Inês smiled. When her daughter was younger, she and João Miguel had had the habit of taking her to the farm once or twice a year, although this now seemed absurd. They would visit Aunt Clarice, that weirdo. Eduarda once overheard that she had just gotten out of a clinic.

Mom, what is that clinic that Aunt Clarice got out of?

It's a beauty clinic, her mother lied. She went to do some skin treatments. Didn't you notice how much prettier she looks?

Eduarda, seven years old, thought it was boring to visit Aunt Clarice because she always looked so downcast, but at the farm there were lots of fun animals, horses and cows and bulls, hens with little yellow chicks (once she drowned half a dozen of them in an inglorious attempt to teach them to swim), dogs and cats, piglets, sheep, a nanny goat. And there were very special people, like the old cook who told scary stories in the kitchen at night. One time she told how she had seen a battle between St. George and the devil, on the top of the hill. She also said there were animal bones that had been left in the middle of the bamboo groves and that on Friday nights the bones came to life and wandered about the pastures, crying out. And she swore that whenever a group of horsemen passed through a gate, the little malicious one-legged Saci-Pererê hopped on behind the last rider. Eduarda was obsessed with these stories, and she always asked to hear them even though they kept her awake afterwards.

As the years went by, however, things changed. One day, the cook who told the scary stories was chopping wood with an axe when a large wood chip flew into her eye and pierced it, and she went blind and quit working. The animals began to disappear, they died off and were not replaced by others. A belated uneasiness began to grow in Maria Inês, an overdue reaction to the facts. At some point, they simply quit making the trips to the farm. Maria Inês agreed with Clarice's wishes to sell a large part of the land because the money invested in the bank paid more than renting it out. And things seemed to take on a definite equilibrium.

The smell of the air and the temperature were already different at *A Parada Predileta*. Perhaps due to the hour of the day, or the day of the week, there weren't any buses in the parking lot nor were there people littering the diner's floor with napkins and straws. A barefoot boy with a runny nose offered to watch the car. Maria Inês and Eduarda were given a piece of paper to register their consumption, which would not be much.

Eduarda would have suggested, in former times, maybe we

could buy something, caramelized milk, a jar of sweets, a guava bar. On that morning, she didn't ask for anything and was quiet. They both went to the bathroom. Maria Inês went first and told Eduarda over the door of the small stall I'll wait for you outside, I'm going to have a coffee.

On the wall next to the old coffee machine was a small poster with the face of John Lennon and the translated lyrics of *Imagine*. Maria Inês squinted her eyes and began to read. *Imagine que não há países. Não é difícil de fazer. Imagine there's no countries. It isn't hard to do.* Next to that, someone had taped a sheet of paper with a hand-written *Prayer to St. Francis. Senhor, fazei-me instrumento de Vossa paz. Lord, make me an instrument of Thy peace.* Maria Inês picked up the dented aluminum coffee pot, filled the porcelain cup with the weak coffee.

The side window at *A Parada Predileta* opened out onto a stream with caramel-colored water. Maria Inês thought about Italy and about Venice and its stinky-sweet-smelling canals. *A tall-short fat-thin man sitting-standing up.*

Eduarda came up and ordered a cup of tea. The waitress poured boiling water into a small coffee pot and put in a teabag that could be anise seed or lemon balm herb.

It all came back to Maria Inês. Maybe she was revisiting it with some new objective, like a writer who picks up a poem written ten, fifteen years earlier and changes a comma, finds a synonym (one she had then looked for in vain), adds a period, substitutes or annihilates a rhyme.

Now she even remembered the exact color of the sweater she was wearing, it was made of wool, it had been fairly cool that day. She remembered the taste of the cocktail she was drinking and above all the good-bad smell that impregnated that late afternoon.

It wasn't their honeymoon, she and João Miguel had been married for four years. But it was one of those luxuries he wanted to have in his life.

Little Eduarda, two and a half years old, had stayed in Brazil under the care of a cousin. Maria Inês had just bought a carnival mask for her and some miniature Murano glass animals. She was happy and decided to buy some postcards, send postcards, why not? Write that she was sitting at the table of a café that had previously been frequented by Casanova, Wagner, Proust. Why not? She stood up happy and multicolored and smoothed her long hair with her hands, the temperature inside her wool sweater was now pleasant. Her smile was comfortable.

She crossed the Piazza San Marco through a multitude of pigeons and went over to the *negozio* that sold postcards and came back almost hopping, very pleased with the photograph on the top of the pile (a canal with dark green water, a building with Moorish windows, a tree with bare branches leaning over a crumbling wall).

There was someone with João Miguel, a very handsome young man. They were talking. Maria Inês came up and was properly introduced, *questa è mia moglie*, Maria Inês, this is Paolo.

Paolo said two or three pleasant sentences that João Miguel translated, then tied everything off with a perfect *ciao*. But Maria Inês caught the look that excluded her: the look exchanged between Paolo and João Miguel. And, no more explicit, the handshake that lasted a second longer than necessary and was a millimeter stronger than a casual handshake.

A stab of pain, nothing more.

It had all started much earlier, but she only discovered it there, on that lovely late afternoon at the Piazza San Marco. And she felt partially guilty. Perhaps João Miguel knew about her. And Tomás.

But she and Tomás had quit seeing each other. Perhaps João Miguel was only getting his *revenge*. Perhaps.

Later Maria Inês had a headache. João Miguel left her to rest in the room at the hotel, they didn't say (never did say) anything about the handsome Paolo, but Maria Inês knew that her husband was going to meet him when he said I think I'm going to take a walk.

My fault, she thought.

Seventeen years later, she realized that her hands no longer clutched the steering wheel as tightly. She began to hum a tune with a determined voice, and Eduarda, puzzled, looked at her because a different song was playing in the car. Then she went back to her magazine.

Maria Inês did not feel slighted. To the contrary. She was now experiencing a loneliness of a different nature, with a different coloration and a different taste. A gentle loneliness, where her deepest doubts became reality. After seventeen years.

She watched the trees zooming past on both sides of the highway and she knew that if she turned off the air conditioning and opened the window she would be able to hear the husky sounds of the locusts outside. Then she explicitly thought about Tomás.

He had arrived on the farm after it all. Otacília and Afonso Olímpio were already dead. They were nothing more than insignificant names carved onto a tombstone in the Jabuticabais cemetery. Clarice's wrists had already been opened and closed. Maria Inês was a physician with her diploma and had given birth to a daughter and that daughter had already grown quite a bit. Everything already occupied specific places that seemed to be definitive, dust was accumulating, silence had settled in. As for himself, Tomás had already made peace with his mediocre career, which was the opposite of sophisticated art galleries, of biennials, of expositions, of panoramas, of retrospectives.

His parents were also no longer alive: they had returned from Chile with the *Abertura,* the transition from the military dictatorship to a civilian democracy, and had died several years later in peace and without dreams. They had lived long enough to fight for *Diretas-já,* the movement for democratic direct voting, and long enough to finally vote for the president of Brazil in 1989. They were still communists. They died communists. And Tomás, who had never become politically militant, surprised himself when he voted for the communist candidate on that November 15th. He remembered all of that now.

He had then broken the rental contract of the small apartment in Rio's Lapa neighborhood, where he lived at the time, close to the steps leading up to the hilly Santa Teresa area, and then his travels began.

His travels were never enough to see all of Brazil. By bus or catching a ride from truck drivers that used unbelievable roads, full of potholes, corroded by time and lack of maintenance. Camping or sleeping in cheap hostels, sometimes bucolic and cozy, but almost always dirty or hostile or indifferent. Selling paintings here and there to finance the next few miles and drawing pastel chalk portraits of smiling tourists. Sinking his feet into the crystalline sand on the beaches, exploring the big cities. Learning the tone of the voice of the forest insects, of the mangroves, of the waterways. Little by little, however, his interest began to wane, like a tired muscle. Or maybe Tomás was simply growing old.

He thought about stopping, of pulling over and turning off the motors, of becoming small (as small as possible). He sold his parents' apartment at a very low price because he wanted to sell it fast and negotiated with Clarice about buying that simple field hand's cottage that had not seen a tenant for years. It could have been somewhere else, in another state, even. A beach in Rio Grande do Norte. Santana do Deserto. The mountains in Rio Grande do Sul. Mato do Tição or Goiás Velho or the backlands of Minas Gerais. But it wasn't somewhere else.

It wasn't unusual for him to tell Clarice about his travels, she enjoyed his stories. That night, while they were waiting for Maria Inês—when they said good-night it was past two—he told her about the Chapada dos Veadeiros plateau and the Araguaia River and also about the Ibitipoca Mountains, which had a national park with imaginative names, Cachoeira da Fada (Fairy Waterfall), Janela do Céu (Heaven's Window), Gruta das Bromélias, Gruta dos Fugitivos (the Bromeliad and Fugitive Caverns). Then he talked about the six months he had lived on the island of Fernando de Noronha, in a house in Vila dos Remédios where a biologist who had come from another country to study the dolphins had also stayed. He'd had an affair with the woman and afterwards they never saw one another again or spoke or wrote. But there lingered in Tomás's memory certain mornings that began very early, before daybreak, when the biologist would take him to observe the movements of the dolphins in the bay.

During all those years that separated the occasion of Afonso Olímpio's death, when they met, and the moment they became neighbors, Clarice and Tomás had not lost touch. They had Maria Inês in common, above all.

There were some other women after Maria Inês, but not many. None of them looked like a Whistler painting, or like any painting for that matter, they didn't even resemble the portraits that Tomás occasionally painted of them. Like the biologist who studied dolphins in Fernando de Noronha.

I think it's odd that you never got married, Clarice said once, and then she added because she thought he deserved an explanation: you know, it's unusual to hit forty without ever having been married, at least once.

One time I lived with a woman, for two years. Does that count as a marriage?

Clarice shrugged. I guess so.

Are you sorry you never had children?, he asked.

I am. But I doubt that I'd have been much of a mother.

Now Tomás was up, it was eight o'clock and the cook Jorgina's guinea fowl went by in a line beneath his window, making their usual racket.

Jorgina lived a few minutes' walk away from Tomás in an old shed that had been transformed into a genuine home, with images of saints taped on the wall, embroidered linen doilies on the furniture, a bed separated from the rest by a curtain, and the occasional visits from grandchildren. Jorgina didn't have a kitchen, but then, she spent most of the day in Tomás's kitchen. Earlier, she hadn't had a bathroom. Jorgina had never lived in a house with a bathroom. She'd had an outhouse built over a stream, it was her bathroom, it had bamboo walls, a thatched roof, no floor and the latrine was the stream itself. Tomás had seen worse, but he had a bathroom built for Jorgina and she'd been grateful to the point that her eyes bashfully filled with tears. At the age of sixty she took a hot shower for the first time in her life.

That morning she made the sweet coffee like she did every day and set the table for Tomás like she did every day, a clean mug, a coffee pot, a pitcher of milk, a saucer with butter, and a baking pan with cornbread. And she watched him as he sat down, he was different, maybe he was sick, had a headache, or had had a nightmare. He drank some coffee without milk and then lit a cigarette and took his time smoking, and stood up, put on his shoes, walked out.

Maybe Tomás was getting old, maybe he had reached that type of plateau where almost all the more intense geographical formations were worn down, maybe he could now look at the view and consider everything to be part of the past.

It was possible that Eduarda was aware of more than met the eye. That she imagined, for example, why João Miguel was so assiduous about his tennis lessons. That was what occurred to Maria Inês when she asked her mother a question with an almost casual tone of voice, as she turned the pages of her magazine and distractedly raised her eyes to watch the scenery go by: and so, are you and Dad going to separate, when we go back?

Maria Inês wasn't surprised. She saw a dog that had been run over lying on the shoulder of the road, the stomach black with coagulated blood, the intestines exposed, and thought someone should move that animal from there, bury it.

Then she answered: yes, maybe.

Eduarda closed the magazine, sighed.

You know, that doesn't make me all that sad. Strange. I don't think that you two have a very good life together. Of course, there are people much worse off. I mean, you don't fight, you don't argue.

Maria Inês simply repeated maybe we'll separate. I don't know yet. I don't know what he thinks about all of this.

Then she thought once more, explicitly, about Tomás.

Nine O'Clock
(Brazilian Daylight Saving Time)

Death in Venice remained in the same spot and the only thing Clarice knew about the book was the very beginning (Prinzregentenstrasse and the rest). Now she recalled a postcard that Maria Inês had sent her from Venice in—1980, '82? The dates were no longer that important (just like in *Death in Venice*: 19 . . .). Nor was the postcard, Clarice had probably thrown it away along with the many things she was always throwing away.

Someone was walking on the road, a man. It looked like Tomás. There were grasshoppers buzzing in the fields. Clarice remembered the fable and how, as a child, she had desperately identified with the ant, and how, today, she would probably identify with the grasshopper. Let winter come. Starve to death, if it was inevitable. But first spend the whole summer singing with the sincerity of grasshoppers and madmen.

The eight o'clock sun (the clock showed nine, Brazilian Daylight Saving Time) was pouring over the hill. On the other side still sat the house (where the many rooms had names) of Ilton Xavier and his widowed mother. He was now the man of the house, the voice of authority. The previous week Clarice had passed by and cordially greeted Roseana, the second and last wife, who was coming down the road holding hands with her small daughter. And she noticed that the house was being painted: always the original colors.

Later she heard that a group of university researchers were preparing a book about the colonial coffee plantations in that region and were going to photograph Ilton Xavier's property. Even though there was not a single coffee plant left there.

Clarice heard the noise of drawers being opened and closed. It was probably Fátima putting away the put-awayable things that were normally scattered about when it wasn't house-cleaning day.

Clarice had spent the rest of the night thinking about her marriage to Ilton Xavier, even if it had meant so little to her, or maybe for that very reason. When Fátima arrived to clean the house, early in the morning, she found Clarice in the garden, picking up the leaves that had fallen off a sycamore tree.

So, today's the big day, she said, imagining that Clarice must be very happy about her sister's arrival. After all those years.

Fátima's hair was decorated with false braids that had taken close to eight hours to weave in and were expensive but a hairdresser friend from Friburgo had done it for free. She had on her work uniform: short, thick cotton shorts revealing her strong, dark, mistreated legs. Blue flip-flops showing toenails polished red, the same color peeling off her short, gnawed fingernails. A cotton knit t-shirt wide at the hem and sleeves, revealing a gray past beneath the bleach stains with the words, Boston, Massachusetts, on the front. Fátima didn't have the slightest notion that it referred to a place—a place in the world, where people also cleaned houses and waited for the arrival of sisters while picking up dry leaves off the ground.

Clarice smiled and tucked a strand of hair that was covering her eyes behind her ear. She was not wearing the same old clay-caked t-shirt, but a dark blue dress with pale blue flowers that made her look meek, placid. So much so that Fátima was sincerely tempted to sit down there for a moment, in the garden, on a rock, and have a conversation. There was work to do, however. Lots of work. Get the house spic-and-span so that Maria Inês and her daughter would not turn up their noses at the past and at the rough grasp of Nature, who ruled over things out there. Fátima wanted to rid the house of all the spiders, do away with the odor of mildew that lurked in some of the rooms and closets, polish the wood to a sheen, remove all the insect corpses from the lamps and light fixtures and from the corners where they accumulated, destroy the ants and the ant beds, soak the bathrooms in eucalyptus and the kitchen in all-purpose cleaner, leave the windows so transparent they would seem to disappear.

Now Maria Inês was on her way. Clarice was surprised to catch herself trying to guess what kind of car she would have. She finally decided on a brand new deluxe imported model, but then felt slightly embarrassed at her own pettiness and searched for some old sentiment that could simply make her happy about her sister's arrival. Happy like by all accounts a sister would be with the arrival of the other sister, a reunion after many years. Easy things, with frank superficiality, visible, audible, and touchable things, things with the face of the noonday sun, of crickets turning green in the bushes, and of cicadas singing their hearts out on tree trunks.

The man that looked like Tomás disappeared along with the highway around a curve.

The January sun was blazing hot, even at eight o'clock, and was almost painful to Clarice's skin when she came out from under the protection of the shadows cast by the trees. Luckily, all around the house they were there, the trees. Some of them had abandoned their status of germinating seed with astonishing speed and were now a miracle composed of trunks and genuine leaves.

Her hair was turning white and she dyed it with Indian henna.

She was forty-eight. She had aged. That was surely the impression Maria Inês would have.

In one month, however, it would be February, the month of Carnival and her birth month. Could she possibly still improvise a few more minutes of acting, given she was still on the stage? Would it be possible to finally reinvent herself in a summer? Now she had practically succeeded in getting rid of any and all expectations. To shrink, curl up like an animal in hibernation. That state of almost-peace would by necessity exclude Maria Inês.

And Maria Inês would come. Why? For what purpose?

The letters written on the beautiful sheets of personalized stationery (a present from Ilton Xavier) began to arrive more often. It was out of the question to openly state the situation (*Mother is dying, come quickly*), but, to the point permitted by a wide-ranging censorship that coated her words like capsules (or like wool slipper socks harboring icy feet on a cold morning), but Clarice was being very insistent.

I think I'm going to have to go there, Maria Inês said to Tomás, while her thin nail-bitten index finger drew a half-moon on his back.

She had started to dress and had put on her panties and miniskirt, but then she lay down again on the bed next to him. Tomás had lit a stick of incense (patchouli) and was eating a chocolate bar while he drew a small elephant with a Bic pen in a notebook. He wore a silver ring on his right hand, a gift from Maria Inês, which he himself had decided to give all kinds of meanings.

She turned over on her back and Tomás watched her small breasts rise and fall with the rhythm of her breathing. Love tightened his chest like a tourniquet. Maria Inês was full of necklaces and bracelets and rings, she had been cultivating a slightly hippie look in her way of dressing. They were listening to rock, an Os Mutantes record. The butt of a joint they had smoked earlier lay yellowed on a saucer.

Of course you have to go, she's your mother, he said.

I don't like her, Maria Inês said, knowing full well those words were untruthful, that they were somehow closer to and beyond the truth.

But she needs you, she's sick. Don't be self-centered.

His tone of voice had the forced niceness of a first grade teacher, slightly tired and dissatisfied with the pay. It upset Maria Inês.

Don't talk to me that way.

But Tomás was gentle, he merely smiled and grabbed her hand to kiss her index finger with the chewed-down nail.

It was the month of October. Clarice and Ilton Xavier were celebrating a wedding anniversary: four years. There was still no heir on the way, much to everyone's dismay.

Saturdays were, at first, the day to have lunch with her parents. As Otacília grew weaker and felt worse, however, the weekly lunch gave way to lunch twice a month and then once a month.

Otacília and Afonso Olímpio were becoming more and more confined to their house and had taken on the aspect of pieces of furniture, so much so that no one believed that they could actually die one day, in spite of Otacília's nameless disease and her iron supplements and vitamins. It seemed only natural to predict that the years would go by, and then the decades, and in sequence, the centuries, without Otacília and Afonso Olímpio changing much—perhaps they would only take on the slightly coppery tone of wood or a gray layer of dusty disuse. But they would continue there, barely breathing, consuming very little air or food, devoid of sleep or smiles. Otacília would sharpen her hearing to listen to the kiskadees and thrushes' singing—which, however, would reveal nothing new. And Afonso Olímpio, having lost his appetite, would regard the table laden with breakfast food and crack his bony knuckles. They would be enemies who, at the end of their lives, had made some sort of a truce.

The truth was, however, that Otacília was dying. There were now lesions on her skin, small baby-girl pink wounds that reminded her of when she was a child running around the yard and falling down. She would sometimes desperately gasp for air and gag on the words in her throat, causing her usual silence to be even more profound and, in a certain way, crueler. It was a silence that used its white inside-out phrases to continually express that whole circle: blame him, Afonso Olímpio, her husband and the father to her two daughters, blame herself. They both probably deserved it, the guilt, even though afterwards reality had changed and taken apparently satisfactory paths. Because stationary things were like volcanoes and not even she, Otacília, or her husband, or her daughters, could expect, with sincerity, that it was all settled.

Maria Inês also knew, with her blazing eyes and her sexual freedom. With her boyfriend Tomás, who now said to her: I think you should go, your mother needs you. Maria Inês would go. To witness Otacília's death, to watch her die.

In the kitchen, Clarice, with her shiny wedding band, was making the *casadinhos* sandwich cookies she had learned to make from her great-aunt Berenice. 3 *cups flour.* 2 *cups sugar.* 6 *yolks.* 3 *egg whites.*

1 teaspoon baking powder. She thought about Lina a bit at the beginning and less later on. *Beat the egg whites until stiff, add the yolks and sugar, beat well and add the flour sifted with the baking powder.*

The taxi arrived just as the *casadinhos* finished baking. She still had to add the filling and frost them, but that would have to wait, it was more important to greet the taxi and its illustrious passenger that had come from the Jabuticabais bus terminal—a small gray bus terminal with parking for two buses and public bathrooms with improvised cardboard boxes on which had been written *tips, thank you*, and with graffiti written on the inside of the stall doors, *Monica and Fábio, Alexandra and Adriano, Only Jesus can save you*. There was also a bar where a handful of inoffensive drunks hung out, circled by a half dozen hungry dogs, hoping for a drumstick bone. And there was a newsstand. The new mayor had surrounded the bus terminal with russet, pink, and yellow bougainvilleas, almost making it cozy.

Maria Inês got off at the bus terminal in a bad mood, but she was better by the time she stepped out of the taxi and retrieved from her hippie purse a hippie wallet (made in India) and from that the payment for the driver. She had begun to tutor science to children and pre-adolescents with bad grades at school: it was *her* money that was paying for the taxi and for the tip.

Clarice waved, happy, and then started giving the kind of excuses she was used to giving even when they weren't necessary: Ilton Xavier's at home, he's expecting the veterinarian who's going there to vaccinate the cattle. I decided to come here to wait for you and bake you some cookies. Mother's asleep.

She did not mention Afonso Olímpio.

How is she?

Bad.

And our father?

He's around, working as usual, the maids say he's been drinking some.

Did he go out?

Clarice nodded while she moved her wedding band from her ring finger to her middle finger and then to her index finger, where it was too tight.

Early this morning. To a cooperative meeting, she said.

Maria Inês put her suitcase and her hippie purse in her bedroom. Clarice noticed how full she was of rings and earrings and necklaces and bracelets. Pretty. She also noticed her flat leather sandals that looked comfortable. Then they both went to the kitchen, to finish making the *casadinhos* and have some *guaraná* soft drink.

Otacília was awake when, half an hour later, her bedroom door opened almost soundlessly and her daughters entered. It was past three o'clock and the October afternoon was cooling down, interrupted by soft, monotonous periods of drizzle. Outside the closed window, seeds triumphed and shoots grew ferociously and multicolored butterflies died and were carried away by ants.

The room smelled like mint tea. Otacília was waiting, eyes open (aquamarine blue with a devastating shine, somewhat feverish), staring at the uneven ceiling. Her daughters didn't notice when her consciousness abandoned her body for a moment and perched on the ceiling, leaving her stark and shallow like a newborn. Then she came to. Maria Inês picked up and held Otacília's hands in her own.

Behind the double bed made of solid jacaranda wood hung a

wooden crucifix and an oil painting depicting a boy with a small dog. A lizard was living behind it and, at night, oblivious to all the rest, devoured mosquitoes and other small insects.

Otacília said she would like to take a bath and fix herself up a bit. Maria Inês and Clarice helped her walk to the bathroom and undress. Her body was terribly thin, her muscles half-atrophied due to so little use. Her breasts were small: the breasts inherited by Maria Inês. Otacília didn't have any scars. But she had all those lesions on her skin that Maria Inês noticed with a start.

They sat her down on the plastic bench that was now always in the shower stall, Otacília was unable to take a bath by herself, or stand up for any length of time. When the good, warm water ran over her thin gray hair, Otacília's mind wandered away for the second time. This time it lasted longer and she firmly believed that she was in the mineral springs resort of São Lourenço, where she had gone on her honeymoon.

Maria Inês and Clarice did not look at each other while they rubbed soap on Otacília and washed her hair with shampoo. But they exchanged some sentences that rang false:

I'll bet those cookies are going to be good.

It's a really good recipe. I learned it from Great-Aunt Berenice, when I lived there.

Oh.

I think I'll go make some tea. Or hot chocolate. How about it?

Great. Let's prepare one of those deluxe afternoon farm teas. I'll make juice and minute rolls.

Clarice then began to enumerate: we have honey, we have guava jelly, we have butter. And *casadinhos*, of course. And a sugar-glazed white cake that Narcisa made yesterday.

We'll all sit at the table.

And wait for Father.

And wait for Father.

Happy.

Happy.

Sweet-smelling.

Sweet-smelling.

Hair all combed.

Hair all combed.

It sounded like they were talking to a child. But it made no difference, because Otacília couldn't hear.

Something very secret and evil moved through the bathroom like a spirit. And it left the bathroom like the spirit of a spirit.

It was not an imported car that brought Maria Inês and Eduarda. But it did have air conditioning. And a CD player where Maria Inês could hear Bernardo Águas singing Monteverdi, or the *Good Will Hunting* soundtrack she had borrowed from Eduarda.

They came up the mountains and arrived in Friburgo with their ears stopped up. Maria Inês once more taught her daughter the unstop-your-ears-maneuver: you hold your nose and blow out strongly.

Eduarda obeyed and became frustrated once more: it's no use, that only stops my ears up even more!

Now swallow.

Eduarda swallowed once, twice.

That doesn't help at all, it's better to yawn.

And she yawned several times. The left ear finally popped, but the right one continued to bother her.

They barely talked for the rest of the trip. The car shook over the numerous speed bumps that were outside the exit from Friburgo. To the left, on the shoulder of the road, at the banks of the river flowing there meager and dirty, were parked trucks selling watermelons, oranges, and tangerines. To the right were furniture stores. Dark, ugly tire repair shops, bakeries. And a huge modern construction that had not been there when, ten years earlier, Maria Inês had last taken that route.

After Friburgo some of the cool mountain air remained behind. But Maria Inês and Eduarda wouldn't know. The air conditioning was working fine. The car was a mobile bubble of European climate traveling through the countryside of the state of Rio de Janeiro in the middle of the summer.

Eduarda's right ear popped all of a sudden.

Oh, finally!

And she withdrew again. To make up or remember a dream, or taste the watermelon, the oranges, and the tangerines that she had not eaten. To intimately be Eduarda, a small and moveable life. And to feed a suspicion that was throbbing in her body. That was growing. Making her nervous, as if she had to read an essay out loud.

Otacília had tea with her two daughters.

She said good afternoon to her husband when he arrived and asked how the meeting at the cooperative had gone, but when he finished answering she no longer remembered what she had asked.

She put on two drops of her precious Chanel No. 5, one behind each ear, before she lay down to rest again.

When that unprecedented tranquility penetrated her room, semi-illuminated by a weak lamp, she knew she was dying.

She heard the voices of her daughters talking, in the room next to hers, Maria Inês's bedroom. Then she heard a little less and felt a dizziness that made her think of a ship on the high seas during a storm. Then the dizziness went away and she opened her eyes and smiled because, in truth, it was all so simple.

Overtime

For Otacília's funeral, her Aunt Berenice rushed in from Rio de Janeiro. It was upsetting when generations subverted time like that, disorganizing it. Nieces dying before the aunts.

It was only after the funeral that Maria Inês called Tomás and told him my mother died.

He complained. You should have told me *yesterday*! I would have gone there.

But she interrupted him and said it wasn't necessary.

It wasn't necessary because João Miguel was there. Her second cousin and his sincere red eyes. With flowers, but, due to the circumstances, without chocolate.

In the small Jabuticabais cemetery, Afonso Olímpio watched the world spin above his head. Inside his head. He had deep circles in the dark skin under his eyes and there were two deep lines framing his mouth. His hair was disheveled and he wore his dark suit badly, although on other occasions it had looked good on him, his custom-made lightweight wool suit.

Afonso Olímpio, next to his enemy daughters. Burying his enemy wife.

Maria Inês stood at his side like a dare. She did not cry, but Clarice cried a lot in the arms of Ilton Xavier, farther off.

When Afonso Olímpio went back home at the end of the afternoon, driving his well-maintained Rural Willys, he did not turn on the lights. He went to the bathroom and urinated and washed his hands and face in the dark. He felt like a desert where the sandy white ground had been blown smooth by the wind. From the big kitchen cabinet (wood painted blue with flowers climbing up the edges of the glass panes and curling around the drawer pulls), he got out a glass. Then he went to the trunk in the living room where he kept, under lock and key, some bottles of hard liquor.

He had whiskey, there, and cachaça. The best home-brewed cachaça from Minas Gerais, brought over from Barbacena. He filled the glass and entered each one of the rooms, a distrustful wolf looking for traps. He caught a whiff of Otacília's perfume, which would outlive her for quite a long time.

He had the impression that someone other than himself sat down at the table to have the vegetable soup that had been prepared by Narcisa, into which he diced yellow cheese and then consumed alternating spoonfuls with bites of bread and butter. And gulps of cachaça. Narcisa saw that he drank, but he didn't care.

Everything began with Otacília and everything ended in her. She was the mute critic and the hateful abettor. The hand that neither strikes nor caresses, but merely rests inert over time and exists in a way that is as indispensible as it is disturbing.

The memory of Otacília ended up being, for Afonso Olímpio, a more bitter and more vivid version of the real Otacília. A half-starved dog that sat at the foot of the table and, with two indecipherable eyes (aquamarine blue), obliged him to face himself. And all the words they had failed to exchange resonated in his ears.

The food did not sit well with him, but he ate it anyway. He had no choice—all his choices were floating in the past. If he looked over his shoulder he could still see them fading away, backwards, already half-immersed in shadows. An idea occurred to him: on what plane of existence are the things that we *didn't* do? What *we could have done, but didn't do?*

In a flash, he understood. A shiver of fear ran through his body. There was, after all, a plane of existence where all the things he had not done were deposited (like money in a bank account). What he could have done. What he should have done. And in his memory the vision of a twelve-year-old girl whose breasts had begun to develop like two small pears beneath her delicate eyelet blouse cried out.

After Otacília's funeral and her secret phone call to Tomás, Maria Inês asked João Miguel to take her for a ride in his car.

I'm not going home now. I don't know where I'm going, she said. And added, without bitterness, as neutral as a sip of water: I don't even know where home is. Is it Great-Aunt Berenice's house in Rio de Janeiro? Is it my father's house on the farm? Is it my sister's house, there with her husband and mother- and father-in-law?

They went from one end of Jabuticabais to the other in a matter of minutes and fled from the town out the back door. Maria Inês's eyes were dry and João Miguel could not understand why.

Where do you want to go?

I don't know. But then she remembered that about seven miles away there was a road to the right and she said go that way.

Her second cousin and future husband obeyed.

She then asked, almost casually: and your father?

Traveling. On business.

As usual.

As usual.

When will he be back?

I don't know. In a week, ten days.

She looked at the road, distorted by the dusky light. She thought of Afonso Olímpio.

The car turned right at the place she indicated.

And now? asked João Miguel.

There's a bridge up ahead. After the bridge, the river flows into a very pretty small lake.

It wasn't all that pretty. She hadn't been there for years, and she remembered it differently. They left the car parked next to a bamboo grove and continued on foot down a steep path. In the distance, the dark bamboo groves looked like enormous hairy insects or giant spider crabs.

João Miguel slipped and fell sitting down, and Maria Inês laughed. He had mud all over the rear end of his slacks. They then arrived at the edge of the muddy, honey-colored lake, burned by the afternoon twilight. Gladiator frogs croaked everywhere and a group of ducks gathered at the margin, a few yards ahead. There were dragonflies buzzing over the surface of the water and the singing of nocturnal birds blended in with the singing of tardy diurnal birds that were probably moving into the night shift. Working overtime.

Maria Inês said there was a time I liked to catch toads to scare you.

Beetles, too, João Miguel added, but they were not smiling like two young adults fondly remembering their childhood tricks.

The kiss did not catch João Miguel by surprise. And the subsequent caresses did not catch Maria Inês by surprise. They were sitting on a low rock in the midst of a group of taller rocks. A huge mango tree was silhouetted against the sky and bats flew from one tree to another, friendly, bewitching, like shallow or indefinite impressions about someplace or someone.

João Miguel did not ask her who the first man in her life had been, nor how many men she had been with. Maria Inês was already (still) an almost twenty-one-year-old woman, and he did not know exactly what sort of stance to take: if with fear or respect, if with admiration or doubt, or simply love. As he proceeded, he realized that her body was not inexperienced. The jealousy that penetrated him like a presence underwent changes as it migrated through his bloodstream, and it reached his heart as a sentiment more confused than jealousy. A bit more possessive, perhaps a bit more destructive—but he had no way of knowing that.

They might have been able to foresee everything right then and there. Venice and the Florian Café. Bernardo Águas. Eduarda. The white apartment in Upper Leblon. The tennis instructor. The Christmas Eves and the profusion of marble. But they were just young adults, more young than adult.

Maria Inês had not planned that, and João Miguel believed, erroneously, that early evening when they made love on an uncomfortable rock at the edge of a honey-colored lake was due to some emotional confusion on the part of Maria Inês, caused by her mother's death. He had no way of knowing that Otacília's death had not caused emotional confusion in Maria Inês. Other things, yes.

Maria Inês lay on top of João Miguel's chest—which had firm muscles and was hairy, unlike Tomás's chest. They remained silent and waited for the first stars to appear, but they did not appear because clouds were gathering and growing thicker. Maria Inês thought the opaque sky looked like a gigantic wound. All of a sudden João Miguel asked her the most improbable question, he wanted to know if it *had been good for her*—that question had never come out of

Tomás's mouth because Tomás preferred to *feel* if it *had been good for her*, and when by chance, he thought it hadn't, he would take the proper measures as meticulously as an artisan and with the passion of a poet. Maria Inês did not want to answer because she herself did not know. Maybe yes, maybe it had *been good*. *Different*, she thought. But he was a different man. She didn't say anything but simply smiled a somewhat confused smile and gave João Miguel two kisses: one on his left eye and the other on his right eye.

When Maria Inês finally arrived home, the grandfather clock showed ten after nine. The lights were all off. Afonso Olímpio was in his bedroom, awake and drunk, and from there he heard her, his greatest enemy, footsteps resonating throughout the house.

Maria Inês's footsteps made noise, now. It was on purpose. However, there were no more cypress seeds to pick up.

The next morning she dressed and packed to travel before even leaving her bedroom to go to the bathroom and wash her face. She went into the dining room with her tote bag on her shoulder, but she did not find Afonso Olímpio.

Narcisa informed her, as she served bread and hot milk: your father asked me to tell you that he had to go out early. He went to see something about the cattle.

Then she left the room, rubbing her eyes that were still filled with tears due to her mistress's death.

Maria Inês picked up a piece of bread and underscored for herself the fact that she was alone, realizing she had rarely been alone in that house. She wished João Miguel was there so they could talk, or silently watch the bee that came in through the window and now executed a slow aerial dance above the colorful, good-smelling table.

And listen to the kiskadees and thrushes, occupied with specific questions concerning their own lives, and totally ignorant of anything else.

João Miguel, however, had left the night before. At the wheel of his car, with the night highway twisting in front of his eyes and the smell of a second cousin fluttering in his hands like a small tame bird. He parked his car for ten minutes in front of *A Parada Predileta*, half-anesthetized by the night, to have a cup of strong coffee, as a precaution. He wasn't sleepy and was still wide awake when he reached Rio de Janeiro, at one thirty in the morning.

The bee examined the table, but managed to find its way out. It was sunny in the yard, in spite of the clouds the night before, and more inviting outside. The purple ipê tree scattered irregular scraps of shade on the ground and insects rapidly sliced through the air, buzzing with their bass-baritone drone. There were purple and white flowers on the purple glory tree and vivid pink blossoms on a low thicket of moss rose plants that had shot up, grown, and spread out on their own—lovely flowers that bloomed in the morning and withered in the afternoon. There were also the short-lived flowers on the hibiscus plants, but these were huge and orange, with a dark center. Maria Inês left the house with her tote bag and her thick hair tied back with a lilac scarf into a ponytail. Hornets were meticulously constructing a new house under the porch roof, and sooner or later Narcisa would destroy their work with a torch like she had done other times, charring their eggs and larvae.

Maria Inês sat on the porch floor, leaning back against the wall. She pulled a pencil and a notebook out of her bag to write a note. *Father, I'm leaving*. She didn't sign the note and left it on the coffee table in the living room under a paperweight. She saw the taxi she had ordered the day before shaking lightly as it crossed over the cattle guard. She said good-bye to Narcisa with a hug that neither asked for nor gave solace, a quick good-bye hug without further meaning.

Do me a favor, Narcisa. Go to Clarice's house. Tell her I had to leave early and I'll write her as soon as I can.

And she got into the cab and closed the door and didn't look back. She didn't see the figure of her father in the distance. She didn't see a scarf with vivid red roses fallen on the road. She firmly believed that she would never again set foot there.

Which might have happened, if it hadn't been for Clarice.

If Clarice had never existed, it would have made a significant difference in their lives, Maria Inês, Otacília, and Afonso Olímpio's. And, nonetheless, she existed, inoffensive, small, obedient, soft-spoken. Hair combed and shoes on her feet. Maria Inês knew that she loved Clarice, she had no doubt about that. But at times her love became aggressive because Maria Inês had lost her innocence too early. Because Clarice suffered. And for that paradox: if Clarice didn't exist, Clarice would not suffer.

Maria Inês thought about her sister in her marital bedroom, combing her hair in front of her dressing table and putting on clean stockings seated on the edge of the bed. She thought about Ilton Xavier whistling while he shaved, in his boxers. She thought about his parents saying the grace at the table before each meal and about obedient Clarice making the sign of the cross, amen, before carefully unfolding her linen napkin. She thought about her mother, now in the Jabuticabais cemetery, whose existence had accomplished its predetermined arc, from nothing to absolutely nothing, and for only a short interval had been concretized in her figure, Otacília. A mother who distributed too few hugs, too few words, and above all, had taken too few stances.

The taxi driver noticed she was crying in the rearview mirror of his old Variant. He felt sorry for her, and the way he found to help was to offer her a mint drop wrapped in green and silver paper.

Maria Inês traveled uncomfortably for hours. The asphalt on the highway was as worn out as a threadbare piece of cloth and the bus that took her from Jabuticabais to Friburgo stank. It smelled like rancid butter and dog hair. From Friburgo to Rio de Janeiro things improved a bit, but not much. When they descended the mountains and hit the lowland, the temperature immediately soared. Through the open bus windows she could hear the sound of the motor, irritating, monotonous, boring.

The seat next to her was empty. On the seat across the narrow aisle, a young mother nursed her baby, which was wrapped in a yellow blanket. A tiny hand escaped from the blanket and held onto its mother's finger while its open eyes received the world that they could perhaps not yet see.

The bus motor growled. Maria Inês clutched her bag and she could smell the exhaust fumes. She closed her eyes and entered into a confused half-asleep state from which she only emerged when the bus had almost reached the Rio-Niterói Bridge. She saw Corcovado Mountain in the distance and the Christ on top, arms wide open. She was returning to the city, to a home that was (also) not hers, to a boyfriend she wasn't in love with, and to the difficult final exams of her second year at the School of Medicine.

Everything was almost the same. That was the most significant piece of evidence.

In the dirty bathroom of the Rio de Janeiro bus station someone had written on the door, with a pen: *Only Jesus can save you.*

Tomás's eyes were fixed on the spot where the trees on the top of the hill were silhouetted against the blue of the sky. They remained open for a considerable time, and Tomás could only close them when he blinked and twin rivulets ran down his face, which he dried with the back of his right hand.

He was walking down the road that had been the road of Maria Inês's childhood. There must be some significance in that.

To be blunt: there must be some significance in everything.

Tomás knew the story. He looked back, in the direction of Clarice's house, and he could see the quarry rising up high in the distance.

A forbidden quarry, which continued serene in its stone existence, in its warm stone respiration, in its soft stone thoughts. Lizards continued to crawl over its skin, and butterflies continued to fly overhead.

Tomás had never had the curiosity or disposition to climb up the high hill and cross the pasture up there, with the river like a gold thread and the animals in the fields like toys, he had not seen the Ipês Farm in its abandonment. These things he only knew from Maria Inês's old stories.

And now he no longer cared. Over the years he had learned the advantages of not carrying around very much—not many books, nor clothes, nor friends, nor many memories.

He lit a cigarette.

Of course he had not always been like that, of course earlier he had been much less wise. And considerably more stubborn. But now he had the sensation that the days going by could not hold any surprises in store for him, if he stayed alert.

No surprises, not even an unfamiliar car that approached before his very eyes, at a slow speed, lurching down the dirt road like a drunk. Not even the moment when the car stopped at his side without turning off the motor, and he could see behind the glass window that slowly rolled down those two women, one very young, the other no longer. One with light blue eyes, so pale they were almost transparent. The other still looking so much like a Whistler painting, in spite of her disguise of short hair and dark glasses.

A Fabulous Ring Bought in Venice

Looking out of his window Tomás could see the sea, to the left, and in the sea a ship moved imperceptibly—it was probable that, to the contrary, it sped right along. When he looked at it again a few minutes later, it was obvious that it had moved, and what to Tomás appeared to be a very small space must correspond to a big chunk of ocean. He imagined the ship's engines running, countless men operating all those motors of huge proportions and water being dislocated beneath the ship's massive body, and he found it odd that at a distance it all appeared to be motionless.

At his window facing Almirante Tamandaré Street, Tomás was now a man of twenty-five, half-torn by personal doubts that his parents had not taught him how to resolve because they were too wrapped up in politics.

He felt his paintings were shriveled like fruit forgotten for a long time in the refrigerator. And as for her, Maria Inês, love and muse, Tomás was afraid he had lost her, without wanting to recognize the fact that he had never had her. But he persevered.

He was now into religious themes. He painted an enormous Madonna with bright colors and a multitude of strokes. An art dealer put the painting in a gallery and it sold at a good price, but Maria Inês was no longer at his side as frequently to share in even these small glories.

I've lost my muse, he wrote to his parents the afternoon the ship imperceptibly crossed that tiny piece of ocean visible from his window. I hope it's only temporary.

It wasn't.

In the Art Deco building, she was writing a letter to Italy at the very moment that Tomás was writing to Chile. An afternoon insulated in January, hot, in which the incessant drone of the cicadas could be heard. Great-Aunt Berenice's cats were scattered about the apartment like kitsch statues, and she drank tea and ate toast and watched television.

That year had everyone separated from one another, at first: Clarice was on the farm, attending to her marriage that was destined to fail. João Miguel was traveling and studying and had begun to cultivate the idea of buying a certain ring for a certain second cousin and proposing an engagement that he did not realize was already stamped and sealed. Afonso Olímpio counted his minutes, counted the grains of sand that fell from the hourglass, and drank away his loneliness. The flowers in the Jabuticabais cemetery once more withered and bloomed as they had always done, since long before the new headstone where that new name, Otacília, was inscribed.

Maybe they were all like the ingredients of a cake or of *casadinhos* sandwich cookies. *3 cups flour. 2 cups sugar. 6 egg yolks. 3 egg whites. 1 teaspoon baking powder.* Maybe there were all a part of an experiment, lab rats in the hands of a god as inventive as he was cruel, as curious as he was sadistic. Or maybe they were nothing at all and had the historical importance of ants drowning in a puddle of rain water.

Perhaps nothing had ever had and nothing would ever have any real importance, and everything that united them was merely a small streak on the wall, a crayon doodle scribbled by a mischievous child.

When João Miguel returned from Italy at the beginning of August, he brought a ring for Maria Inês in his baggage. It was at the farm where they met again, but not at her father's house for Maria Inês was staying with Clarice. Afonso Olímpio was dead and his funeral had been a month and a half earlier.

I'm so sorry, Maria Inês. He hugged her and was angry with himself because when he passed his hands down her back and noticed she was not wearing a bra a spark flared in the center of his body. It was not the time for such things.

It was so soon, he said, with a condolatory voice. I mean, between your mother and him. Less than a year.

He was drinking too much, she said.

That was all she was willing to reveal to João Miguel.

The ring had been purchased in Venice—the city where there was a certain Café Florian. Of Proust, Casanova, and Wagner. It had been expensive like everything in Venice. It was in João Miguel's suitcase, in its limbo of dark blue velvet, awaiting Maria Inês's *yes*, dreaming about the ring finger on her left hand.

I suppose no one was expecting it, he said.

I was expecting it, Maria Inês interrupted him. You have no idea what he was like. Destroyed. A drunk.

You shouldn't talk about your own father like that.

She didn't answer.

João Miguel didn't notice that Maria Inês's words carried no anger or resentment, they only spoke the truth.

They were walking arm in arm through the gardens of the

house. Clarice was seated on a bench in front of a small oval lake with a fountain that was temporarily mute. Her curved back formed a perfect arc in her old burgundy wool sweater and she was looking down at her feet.

There were no affinities—and never would be—between her and João Miguel. Even so he felt obliged to speak to her, of course, and pull out some sentence from his etiquette manual and state it with his condolatory voice, which was what he did, and they both felt no need for further actions or words. Then Clarice and Maria Inês exchanged glances that crossed in the air like needlepoint stitches. João Miguel didn't notice.

The winter morning was of a timid blue. There were no clouds in the sky, but the splotches of sun on the ground were weak, it was cold. The previous day, in the early morning, the thermometer that Ilton Xavier had placed outside the window had registered thirty-nine degrees. Maria Inês's thin, pale fingers enjoyed the contact with João Miguel's sweater.

We're going to take a walk, she told Clarice. Do you want to join us?

She shook her head while barely smiling. And kept turning her wedding band on her finger shrunken by the cold air.

Maria Inês and João Miguel left the garden through the small side gate where only one person could pass at a time. They went down five concrete steps to the curved path surrounded by thickets of balsam plants that led to the main highway. Always the same dirt road that threatened to soil João Miguel's beautiful Italian shoes—patent leather, shiny, reflecting the day's light.

Now you've come back to stay, she said in an affirmative tone, as if she didn't want to entertain any doubts.

Yes, I'm home for good, he answered.

They passed by the primitive wood cottage raised off the ground on four pilings, where empty milk cans waited to be filled the next morning for the cooperative truck to pick up and exchange for new empty ones. Cows with swollen teats grazed in the pasture and warmed themselves in the sun. They were motionless, except for their tails that chased away horseflies and botflies.

The winter insects were the ticks. João Miguel knew that the pasture was full of them, that the grass seethed with their small, unmerciful lives.

A boy about ten years old passed by, wearing black galoshes, shorts, and a very old, light blue wool sweater that had unraveled at the bottom and been rewoven with wool of another color. His nose ran and he cleaned it with the sleeve of his sweater. His right arm carried a hoe resting on his shoulder. He walked by, greeted them. Morning. Morning, Maria Inês answered.

They saw a white guira rise up in flight from some brush. Two, three, five birds followed it. The guiras always flew in flocks.

Maria Inés and João Miguel returned to the house shortly before lunchtime and found Clarice in the kitchen, helping her mother-in-law and the servants. Grating coconut for the *quindim* pudding. They were all semi-mute, as if words of any type might desecrate that double mourning, the mother and the father of those two girls in an interval of less than a year, poor things.

Less than a year would also be the time that Clarice would need for the events to ferment inside her and to turn into wine, vinegar, or simply a common rotten mixture that no one would perceive, as in fact no one did perceive.

In that August of mourning, however, she was still docile demure submissive well-mannered polite discreet adorable. She did not drink and she did not snort coke, she merely grated coconut for the *quindim*. A black cat with a white chest and face sat next to the wood-burning stove and licked its right paw. Later that same day she called her sister and asked the favor: Maria Inês, maybe you could take care of the inventory for me. You and João Miguel, after all he's a lawyer.

Of course, of course we can, Maria Inês answered.

After all, João Miguel was a lawyer. And he had just asked for her hand in marriage with a fabulous ring bought in Venice.

It was not Maria Inês who told Tomás about Afonso Olímpio's death, but Great-Aunt Berenice, between sobs that shook her cheeks and the soft rolls of fat on her double chin. He caught a bus and went to Friburgo and there he caught another bus that took him to Jabuticabais after making stops in a dozen bus stations of small towns that were also not on the map. In Jabuticabais he took an unmarked taxi that took him to the farm.

He met Clarice for the first time at the wake. She was sitting by herself on the last step going up from the main street of Jabuticabais (the only one paved with cobblestones) to the door of the church. Inside, in the chapel, a small crowd surrounded the coffin that held Afonso Olímpio's body.

The coffin was closed. Nothing could be seen, not the crushed hands. Nor the expressionless face, nor the cracked skull or the fractured limbs. The people were obliged to believe that there was a corpse inside and that the corpse *was* Afonso Olímpio.

When Tomás saw Clarice that first time, she was sitting there on the step in front of the church. She was wearing a black old lady dress and buckled shoes without stockings and her black hair was pulled back into a bun. Her face, in contrast, was mortally drained of color—an irregular paleness composed of shadows here and there, almost like light bruises. She didn't have on dark glasses, so Tomás could see her eyes, and they were dry.

Maria Inês was approaching her sister when she noticed Tomás going up the steps. Your great-aunt told me, he explained.

For an instant the three of them looked at each other. They would only meet again, the three together, twenty years later (while Eduarda slept in the bedroom and João Miguel slept in his seat thirty-five thousand feet in the air).

A stork flew over them, a low flight of wide slow wings. Then a very fine drizzle that seemed to be composed more of dust than of drops of water came down from all directions.

This is Clarice, my sister, Maria Inês said. Her voice low, hoarse, a contralto's voice. Clarice, this is Tomás, whom I've told you about.

They went inside.

The chapel smelled of roses and the odor was dense, present, and made the air difficult to breathe. Some relative was reading a prayer and immediately afterwards another began an emotional speech praising the qualities of Afonso Olímpio. Good husband, dedicated father, the man said. They buried Afonso Olímpio next to Otacília and later decorated the headstone with an oval photograph of the two together.

When I die, bury me far away from here, Maria Inês said to Tomás. But he did not have even a momentary illusion that she was planning for them to have a life in common. A woman whom he loved desperately, painfully.

He returned to Rio that same afternoon. They offered him a

place to stay, but he didn't consider staying. He was dejected, bitter, disappointed. And somewhat frightened as well.

When she returned to her great-aunt Berenice's apartment, in the Flamengo neighborhood, so close to the sea, Maria Inês was wearing her engagement ring, and she went after Tomás to tell him.

He felt diminished. And said I was imagining this would happen. Then he added, with a touch of self-pity, however, there were times I truly believed you liked me.

She didn't answer. She hurriedly mumbled some inanities. She cried a little and explained that she had known João Miguel since she was a child—but she reassured Tomás that yes, he had been the first man in her life. He commented, bitterly, that apparently that fact was not so important. She went to the bathroom to blow her nose and he followed her and leaned against the door, his arms crossed, looking at her.

Does any of this have anything to do with your parents' deaths?

No, she lied.

So you mean to say you like this cousin of yours.

Yes.

You love him.

Yes. Look here, Tomás, you and I know each other well enough for me to be able to guess that it wouldn't work out, she said, and he thought that to be a hollow affirmation.

While she repeated herself, he let his thoughts fly and imagined how it would be, for example, the next night. Definitively without Maria Inês. After five years. A first night in which he would not find any alternative to getting drunk, and perhaps telephone his parents—or, better still (worse still), some available female friend.

A guy he knew had once pronounced that rude, ironic maxim: to cure a Platonic love, nothing better than a Homeric fuck. Tomás smiled to himself on thinking that, and his heart relaxed a touch. And he accepted it.

They tacked their conversation together with some false trivial preoccupations. She said I wish you all the success in your career, and he said I hope you'll be happy—the most commonplace platitude he could find in his stock. Then she added, with a let's-be-friends-forever face: invite me to your exposition, okay? And he said okay, imitating her while lightly making fun of her: and you invite me to your graduation, okay?

The graduation where she would wear a genuine emerald ring. As she now wore that fabulous ring bought in Venice by her second cousin and future husband (for better, for worse, in sickness and in health) João Miguel.

Maria Inês asked for a glass of water and went with Tomás to the kitchen. She drank little, less than half. And she stood there for some time with the glass in her right hand, at the height of her face, studying the little red strawberries painted on the glass. The gesture made her slightly cross-eyed, which Tomás noticed with an unbearable fondness.

When they went back to the living room, she took advantage of the proximity of the front door and stopped and said look, so I'd better get going.

Tomás froze. She opened the door herself, took three steps to the elevator and pushed the button. She watched the numbers light up, 1, 2, 3, 4, 5, 6, on the recently polished panel, bright yellow, smelling like Brasso. She imagined the doorman with a yellow dust cloth working there, up on a ladder. Then she looked at Tomás, who was still motionless, and opened the elevator door and left, saying good-bye with an overly artificial smile. A tutti-frutti chewing gum smile.

Tomás remained motionless for more than one minute, more than two minutes, looking at the empty hall and seeing the numbers light up and carry Maria Inês away, to the world, to the open sea. 6, 5, 4, 3, 2, 1. In a countdown.

Maria Inês left, but not definitively. She came back months later, and continued to come back over the next two years. A clandestine Maria Inês that later would blame herself and believe that the handsome Paolo in Venice was just a type of tradeoff. A girl who still looked like a Whistler painting, in spite of everything.

The wedding was in December, after an engagement that was so brief it only lasted long enough to order the beautiful invitations with embossed names. And the slanting script of *in memoriam* written under the names of her parents and also under the name of his mother. The *vecchio* Azzopardi was the only survivor, in truth the only one with the right to be inviting anyone to anything. Knowing that, and knowing who he was, the guests responded with expensive presents and with a massive turnout.

Maria Inês and João Miguel, at the Outeiro Church. She looked nothing like the Carnivalesque bride that Clarice had been. She had become a proper lady overnight, and her dress was elegant and understated, as was the entire ceremony and the ensuing reception.

To help them get a start in life, the *vecchio* Azzopardi gave them an apartment as a gift. Not yet in Alto Leblon, but in Laranjeiras, on General Glicério Street, in front of a family of trees. Three bedrooms, one for the couple, another for the future sons and the other for the future daughters. He also gave them airplane tickets to New York, where there was a hotel room on the Upper East Side reserved for a week. And a handful of dollars to spend, at musicals, at plays, in restaurants, in Fifth Avenue shops. He then closed the floodgates, because he thought that making it too easy for young people could spoil them and weaken that part of them they needed to fuel their engines for hardships and struggles. And he told João Miguel that the office would be expecting him back two weeks after the wedding, no longer.

The Whistler girl returned to Tomás on a humid afternoon that made his hands and bare feet cold and sticky. There was now a wedding band on her left hand. And also a new watch.

She had once and for all abandoned her earlier persona. She now took care of an apartment on General Glicério and drove a car. On the afternoon she came back, Tomás's first impulse was to send her away and to lock her outside of himself like an inside-out safe.

It was then, however, that she spoke. For an entire uninterrupted hour she spoke and told a story that had begun on a day long before when cypress seeds had spilled from her hands. The day that she had stopped being a child, due to what she had seen.

Her father, her sister.

And Maria Inês continued with the story, and after hearing it, Tomás would also never be the same. But he took Maria Inês in and he enveloped her in his arms with his sad, incomplete love. One more time.

Ariadne's Thread

A part of Clarice liked to belittle Maria Inês's image just a tad, which she did in direct proportion to the sophistication of her sister's material possessions, but the car that rolled up in a whisper, well into the morning, was not a sophisticated one. It was a middle-class car, a metallic green that reflected the sunlight. But Clarice thought, implacable in spite of herself, Maria Inês's husband must have another one, maybe one of those huge SUVs that soccer players, soap stars, and pop singers always bought when they got rich.

There she was, thinking about cars. Clarice felt ashamed of herself and went to greet her sister and niece with hugs that attempted to be blank pages, smooth, fresh embraces.

They exchanged standard greetings precisely because those are the ones that tend to flourish at times when sincerity runs the risk of becoming mushy. How was the trip? Fine, thanks, wow, it looks so different, the trees have grown so much. You look great. Well thanks, you, too. What a long time. I'll say. Heavens, look how Eduarda's grown. Don't you want to come in? Bring in your luggage? I'll go call Fátima, she's dying to see the two of you.

Maria Inês stopped for a moment on the porch, to catch her breath before entering the house. On the red cement floor there was a small crack that ran like a meandering river from the outside wall to the grass in the yard. In the space of the crack small plants grew a half inch, an inch high, a miniature forest for the spiders and ants.

She didn't turn around to face Clarice when she said we ran into Tomás on the road. She made an effort to make that sentence sound casual and stood looking around, her hands on her hips, then added, it's incredible how men age better than we do.

Eduarda was squatting and petting a small poodle, with a coat the color of honey. It was hard to know if that was its original color or the result of years of dirt soaked into its hair.

Fátima appeared at the door, drying her hands on her shirt (Boston, Massachusetts), and hopped in circles around Maria Inês and Eduarda as if she herself were a puppy. She gave Eduarda a big hug and said my goodness, the last time I saw this girl. How old were you, honey? About eight? Nine? Come on in, everybody, please! Let me get your luggage.

She had baked a marble cake and made fresh drip coffee and a pitcher of pitanga juice, which she proceeded to set out on the table.

It seemed unbelievable that everything was still there. The mustard-colored recliner, the fireplace with logs piled in front, the iron poker hanging on its iron base. The same rug and, on the wall, the same photograph of Otacília in her wedding dress. Clarice's presence all those years had barely made a dent. There was only one indication discernible: the Thomas Mann book on the coffee table, *Death in Venice*.

Maria Inês said *Death in Venice* out loud while she thought of the book she'd never read and remembered the Piazza San Marco full of pigeons and a *negozio* that sold postcards.

I'm trying to read it, said Clarice. But I can't seem to concentrate much these days. Have you read it?

Maria Inês said no, and she continued to look around. Everything the same, everything different. The house was like the sensation that she herself, Maria Inês, felt after a migraine headache crisis: an empty relief, an amplified absence of pain. A bad feeling that goes away and takes all the good feelings with it and leaves a gap in its wake.

She and her daughter went to their rooms. Maria Inês would stay in the room that, in the past, had been the guest room and Eduarda, in the one that had once been Maria Inês's room (and where Clarice would go to spend the rest of the night). Everything the same, everything different.

Butterflies still flew over the quarry. But there was no one around to decree it off limits. The Ipês Farm had been sold three years earlier and divided into four smaller pieces of property. One was a study center for alternative medicine. If she were to decide to go up to the quarry at that very moment, Maria Inês would no longer see ghosts writhing inside the abandoned house, but people robed in white, burning incense, intoning out-of-tune mantras on the well-manicured lawn.

She did not, however, intend to go up to the quarry. She left her bag on top of the bed covered with the patchwork quilt that Otacília had made years before, before she ever got sick, and cast a furtive eye out the window, as if she were afraid of what she might find there. She found nothing other than the yard all grown up, already an adult, needing a few repairs perhaps, some tree trimming, a little revamping. There were three fairly tall sycamore trees with small piles of dried leaves near their trunks.

She then went to the bathroom, which was the only one for the four bedrooms. There were no suites with white bathrooms filled with ornamental gardens; it was a simple mid-sized farmhouse. Maria Inês looked at herself in the mirror and got mascara and kohl eyeliner out of her purse and retouched her eyes. She washed her hands with a green heart-shaped soap that smelled like cheap motel soap (thanks to Bernardo Águas, she was very familiar with the odor of motel soap).

When she went back to the living area, her sister and her daughter were already sitting at the table drinking juice.

Eduarda, her back to her, was in the chair Afonso Olímpio used to occupy. Maria Inês looked at Clarice and she felt something similar to a hiccup in her heart, but she then decided it had all been worth it. Because, after all, Clarice had survived.

She joined them at the table and poured some coffee into a cup. She knew the coffee was too sweet, but it didn't matter.

Outside, a man was killing time by walking down the dusty road.

Outside, there were new birds singing old melodies.

Clarice played with her wedding band, where the name *Ilton Xavier* could be read on the inside. The windows were closed because it was that time of day when the mosquitoes began to invade the house. She had to be careful so that she would sleep peacefully, later on. Without mosquitoes, without thoughts.

In a few weeks they would begin to harvest the corn. Clarice smiled, the wedding band was spinning like a top between the surface of her dressing table and the pad of her index finger. *Roda pião, bambeia pião. Spin, top, spin, wobble, top.* Her husband and his parents had gone to church.

I'm not going, I'm so sorry, I have a terrible headache.

Adorable Clarice. Understandable, forgivable. I love you because you don't have any secrets, Ilton Xavier once said.

Everything danced in a confused ring-around-the-rosy in her memory. The afternoon Maria Inês dropped all her cypress seeds, her precious cypress seeds, the five long years in Rio de Janeiro at Great-Aunt Berenice's home, and her childhood friends and the young girl named Lina, the letters to Ilton Xavier, the marriage to Ilton Xavier and her wedding night in which her body and his body were on fire for different reasons. And the bottles of alcohol that followed, such refined liqueurs, such friendly brandies, wines, whiskey. Anesthetics, pleasant like a breeze in the late afternoon.

It was shortly after her birthday, in February, during the first summer after her father's death. Clarice went into her bedroom and sat in front of the mirror. She looked the same. Then she remembered Lina and her scarf with faded roses dirtied with mud.

Ilton Xavier was not at home, nor were his parents. Clarice had just had her breakfast alone at the immense jacaranda wood table built by slaves in the nineteenth century. And she had wandered about the old plantation house for a while, passing a servant sweeping the hardwood flooring here and there.

Her bedroom had not yet been straightened and the tall windows were still closed. Clarice did not turn on the lights, she did not open the windows. She saw her shadow-filled face reflected in the dressing table mirror. She took her wedding band off her ring finger and moved it to her middle finger, to her index finger, where it fit snuggly. To her thumb, where it fit only halfway down. Then she left it on the dressing table, between a bottle of cologne and a jar of face powder.

It was time. Clarice opened the armoire and chose some pieces of clothing, just a few. She could hear Otacília's voice saying two suitcases, but she only got one, and she got some money, as well, without counting the amount. Her shoes made a rhythmic sound on the endless hardwood floors.

She went over to the chest of drawers where a dark bottle rested on top. Ilton Xavier had drunk one or two glasses, the night before, while reading some book. The fragile crystal cordial glass, so breakable, still had a small coffee-with-milk-colored circle in the bottom. She picked up the bottle and read *Irish Cream*. She poured some into the glass and drank.

Before leaving the bedroom, she picked up her wedding band and placed it in the pocket of her blouse. She stepped into the bathroom and lifted the toilet seat and kneeled down on the floor and vomited. Her eyes filled with tears she did not want, tears that were not for Ilton Xavier nor for her marriage that was now coming to an end. Nor for the children that she had not had, nor for Lina.

Then she left. The maid saw her pass by carrying a small suitcase. She stared and then ran to the kitchen to tell the others. In the meantime, Clarice stopped a farmhand in the yard, and requested: Duílio, please do me a favor, hook up the buggy and take me to Jabuticabais.

Duílio complied and Clarice did not utter a word the whole way and when they reached town she dispensed him with a tip and shook his hand.

Go on, Duílio, I know you still have a lot of work to do.

And how will you get back, ma'am?

I'll catch a cab later, Clarice lied. She never went back.

The town smelled like sunshine. It was already ten o'clock. She walked to the bus station carrying the suitcase and feeling the sweat dampen her temples and the nape of her neck. She bought a ticket for the bus to Friburgo that would leave at eleven thirty, then she went to the tree-lined square and sat on one of the green benches that surrounded the bandstand. To wait.

To wait and to look at her own hands with disgust, then with pity, then with love. She could not disassociate herself to be able to understand the story in a different way. She was at the same time witness, victim, and executioner.

She was Clarice, who never should have been born, who had ruined one family and was now ruining another. But of course that was merely one of the many ways to look at things.

The bus bounced wildly along the way and Clarice felt like vomiting again and, since there was no bathroom, she had to use a plastic bag. The passenger sitting in front of her turned around and shot her a look of disapproval. She cleaned her mouth with a handkerchief she had in her purse, white, chambray linen, embroidered with her initials, a present from Ilton Xavier.

She no longer knew what time it was when she got off in Friburgo. She wasn't thinking about lunch, but she was thirsty. She entered a bakery and asked for a bottle of sparkling mineral water. She drank it, but she continued to feel empty and light-headed. And so separate from everything as if she were a ghost. For a moment she had the impression that if she were to touch the glass of the counter her hand would go right through it.

At that moment a landowner from the Jabuticabais region came into the bakery, saw Clarice, and went up to greet her.

Good afternoon, Dona Clarice. Are you alone?

With effort she nodded, forced a smile on her face, and gave him a reasonable explanation, saying I've come in to do some shopping.

He laughed and said well you probably did well to come alone, my wife says we husbands only get in the way when it comes to shopping.

He then kissed her hand, good shopping, my best to your husband and his parents.

She stood watching the man leave. In the next instant, as if a meticulous filmmaker were directing the scene, she heard a voice behind her. I know you, said the voice, and Clarice turned around to see who was talking. A woman who should have been pretty, but now hid her beauty like a secret behind her deep circles, her frightening thinness, her ill-fitting clothes.

The woman slowly took a drag off her cigarette, exhaled, and took a sip of her soft drink. You're Otacília and Afonso Olímpio's daughter. From the Santo Antônio Farm.

Clarice fixed her eyes on the soft drink bottle and thought about its slogan: *Grapette, Thirsty or Not.* She wanted to say something, but only managed to sigh. Her head was beginning to ache.

You look like you're feeling terrible, said the other woman. And you don't remember me, of course.

Grapette, Thirsty or Not.

She came closer.

I'm Lindaflor, you surely remember the Ipês Farm. Jesus, you're green, girl! Have a sip of this.

Clarice said no, thank you, I just arrived on the bus and I'm feeling a little queasy. I'm sorry if I didn't recognize you, I think I was very small the last time we saw each other.

I was, too, but you haven't changed a bit. You still have a baby face. Oh, sorry, I didn't mean that as an offense, I think it's cool. We must be more or less the same age, and just look at me. All worn out. You had a younger sister.

She's living in Rio. She got married two months ago.

And you're married, too.

Yes. But I'm separating from my husband today.

God damn, that explains your face. Where are you going to stay, here in Friburgo?

I don't know. I need to find a cheap hotel. Maybe a boarding house.

Grapette, Thirsty or not.

And why don't you go to Rio, stay with your sister?

I don't like her husband. And he doesn't like me. And, anyway, I need to get away from her for a while as well.

And your parents?

They're dead. My father last year. My mother two years ago.

I get it. A change of scenery, right? Listen, I know a nice boarding house on my street. Do you want me to take you there?

Lindaflor did not wait for an answer and took some wadded bills out of her purse to pay for the Grapette and gave Clarice a sweet, tired smile.

At that exact instant Clarice embarked on a downward curve towards the precise, sharp redemption of an Olfa knife found on top of an old wooden table where someone had written with a blue ballpoint pen: *Ronaldo loves Viviane*. Where there was also a piece of hard, stale bread on a plastic plate and a leaf-shaped glass ashtray overflowing with cigarette butts and a pornographic magazine with the cover exhibiting a busty blonde with parted lips, in leather boots, sitting astride a Harley-Davidson.

Clarice only sent news to Ilton Xavier a week after leaving him. She didn't write on her sophisticated personalized stationery because she had not taken it with her. Her words emerged from a common ballpoint pen and poured onto cheap notepad sheets that were subsequently folded three times and sealed in a long airmail envelope with green and yellow borders. A letter to Ilton Xavier and an almost identical letter to Maria Inês.

She said she wanted to be alone, for that reason she was not going to send her address, but she was fine. She badly needed to sort out some personal matters.

Maria Inês knew what those matters were, Ilton Xavier did not. He concluded it was about another man and was furious, he separated everything that Clarice had left behind and filled two boxes and had them sent to Maria Inês's house in Rio de Janeiro. Later he forgave her, because that was his nature, and he remarried and had a houseful of children and was happy and even bought the red pickup of his dreams.

Clarice became friends with Lindaflor, who in turn introduced her to the many friends she had in Friburgo and environs. They stayed for a while at the house of one of those friends in the nearby village of Lumiar, where they smoked pot all day and every now and then looked for mushrooms to make tea. They told Clarice that those were simply ways to enter into other-levels-of-consciousness (like in the Carlos Castañeda books. *Journey to Ixtlan*, got it?). Later she also discovered that cocaine was good for making her feel intense and for making the world shine. And alcohol was the anesthetic.

All of those things, however, cost money. So she would get jobs that didn't last long: first as a receptionist for an English language school, then as a salesperson in a shoe store, then as kitchen help in a German restaurant where she learned how to prepare *Wurtz mit Kartoffelsalat und Rotkohl*.

At one point, it became too expensive to live in a boarding

house. She spent five months living with Lindaflor in Friburgo, then she moved to the town of Cordeiro, where she had a friend who needed someone to take care of her daughter. She stayed there for almost a year. She immediately thereafter ended up in Niterói, then went back to Friburgo and tried selling her sculptures in Teresópolis.

Until, finally, she lost track of everything. She met up with a man who took her to a dark room in a boarding house in a poor neighborhood in Rio. It made no difference where she was. He bought whiskey for Clarice and there was always cocaine. Sometimes he would disappear for three or four days, but he always came back. Once he brought her a cat as a present, but the cat ran away, maybe because they didn't give it enough food. Then, one day, Clarice found the knife.

She was thirty-eight years old. And there were no more windows-to-shut-because-of-the-mosquitoes. She wasn't quite sure where she was, but the guy standing at the door was some sort of protector that entered her body (she barely felt it) and brought her the bare necessities: booze and cocaine. That wedding band (*Spin, top, spin*) had long been sold, it brought in some decent money, it was top-quality gold.

Ilton Xavier and his parents must be at church. She didn't know, it didn't matter.

Time had passed by, it was true, but now Clarice had the impression that she had lost her references: a labyrinth without Ariadne's thread. A vast dark tunnel. It was true that she didn't *think* so much now, in the sense that her brain had become velvety, that was good, but it was also true the old pain was still there, sharper and bottomless.

In the years prior to 1500, the Portuguese ships were exploring the Atlantic Ocean. Clarice remembered some history class although she couldn't remember the teacher's face. She imagined the immense sails hoisted, and she herself felt like a ship, or a caravel—she was now in the middle of the ocean, there were terrible storms and desolate calms, hunger, thirst, and illnesses, nothing to do except *pray*, but Clarice did not feel like praying because she was very, very tired. Wherever she looked, there was only the sea, the immense ocean.

A drag off her cigarette. The man took off her clothes and she barely felt it. The dark room and his hands on her scrawny haunches with pointy bones that jutted out aggressively in her jeans. After half an hour the man left, said he was going to buy some food. Clarice had a plastic smile on her lips that didn't belong to her, as if she had stolen a smile from someone else and now displayed it, like a pair of earrings or a purse. That idiotic smile remained there, hanging on her face, even after it was no longer necessary.

The man left. She was thirty-eight.

Someone has a canary in a nearby apartment and the little creature sounds like it's going to sing until it bursts. Desperate, it sings to attract the female that will never come because female canaries don't normally nest with caged males. Even if one of them is flying unawares through the neighborhood, which is very improbable. Some woman with a powerful voice sings while she washes dishes in her kitchen. Clarice hears the plates hitting against one another. Then a child whines and the woman with the powerful voice lets out a curse word. And the canary continues to sing.

The knife is on the old wooden table where someone has written with a blue ballpoint pen: *Ronaldo loves Viviane*. There is also a piece of hard, stale bread on a plastic plate. A leaf-shaped glass ashtray overflowing with cigarette butts and a pornographic magazine with the cover exhibiting a busty blonde with parted lips, in leather boots, sitting astride a Harley-Davidson. On the ceiling a fan rotates lazily, it can't even agitate the air that smells like mildew and tobacco.

There is a white porcelain bathtub (filthy) in the bathroom because there is always a bathtub for these occasions.

Clarice spins above herself. When the sharp blade lacerates the flesh of her wrists, Clarice smiles. The blood staining the bathtub water is the element of a very personal communion.

She calmly closes her eyes. On top of the table, right on top of the pornographic magazine, a fly lands, and ambles between the breasts of the busty blonde, over the Harley-Davidson wheels, then eats some breadcrumbs.

The emerald ring was so beautiful. It came nestled in a small box covered in dark blue velvet, so that it would look like the engagement ring, which she had received only a few years earlier.

Maria Inês wore a lovely red dress for her graduation, a color that flattered her fair skin and the dark, dense shadow of her hair. A *Symphony in Red*. When she walked up to receive her diploma the two men in her life observed her and tried futilely to predict the future.

In the arms of her nanny, a sleepy one-year-and-a-few-months-old Eduarda played with the pink ribbon that attached her pacifier to her dress. Tomás was close enough to see the child with her white stockings and her white patent-leather shoes, a ribbon bow on each one. The curls of her light, fine hair were held back with a white headband, and she wore the dress of a princess, pink. Her cloth doll, and a big bag where the bottles and diapers must be, lay on the chair. The nanny softly rocked back and forth and Eduarda's eyes began to close, they became two small strands of attention, then they gave themselves up to sleep.

Next to her was João Miguel, whom Tomás had never met until then. The second cousin and the husband of his lover, or perhaps things should be arranged in a different hierarchy.

Little Eduarda sighed deeply, which Tomás could not hear but surmised from the movement of her chest, a small arch up, then down. In the meantime her mother, Dr. Maria Inês, held her rolled-up diploma with the hand where her splendid emerald sparkled.

Tomás noticed once more, with aching affection, that her belly had become slightly protuberant after her pregnancy, which made her body more beautiful. Her hips were also a bit wider beneath her dress.

Eight years: that was how long that delusion had lasted. Just because once he had decided to compare her to a Whistler painting and sketch her and call to her from the window of his apartment. A girl who was now married and had a daughter and a diploma and a genuine emerald ring.

Tomás gave up trying to predict the future. The future was today. Yesterday, perhaps. The future was running late, or, better put, he was running late for his future. Because *time stands still, but creatures pass by*.

He looked at his watch, it was twelve past seven. And Maria Inês beautiful, with the body of a mother making her even more beautiful in that red dress. Her husband in the audience, in a navy blue suit. Her daughter in the audience, a pink princess asleep in the arms of her nanny.

It was then that Tomás realized that their story was dead and buried. At seven-twelve. He caught a glimpse of a still-young man who had dedicated himself to the illusion of a woman. He looked at the man named Tomás and looked at the woman whom he had continued to meet even after her marriage and he looked at the child asleep in her nanny's lap. A pink princess. A red queen. And he, the frog-prince.

He felt ill. Something grabbed hold of his stomach. He stood up from his seat and he squeezed past several pairs of knees and reached the aisle that led out of the auditorium. The aisle was covered with a red carpet—a red carpet for a red queen. Tomás felt her eyes on his back, penetrating like knives, and they hurt. He thought he should turn around and bow, like making the sign of the cross when leaving church.

He didn't turn around and he didn't see Maria Inês again in her beautiful mother's body and the tiny Eduarda with her head resting on her nanny's shoulder. He walked out at a very fast pace, thinking he would not be able to control the spasms in his stomach.

And that was it. Maria Inês saw the massive door of the auditorium open and close and she heard the city sounds swallow up Tomás. He was abandoning her, years after she had abandoned him.

Thirteen Years and Fourteen Summers

Once upon a time there was a butterfly that ripped the fresh mountain air and danced above a forbidden quarry where gray lizards warmed themselves in the sun. In the routine path of its flight, the butterfly could see, to one side, an abandoned farm and a house with plants growing on the roof. To the other side, a farm with animals in the pasture that looked like toys and a river that was a long golden thread.

On the banks of the river were four children. The oldest was named Lina and she was still not in danger. She had not yet received that hand-me-down scarf with faded red roses and her hair sparkled in the sunlight. Small drops of water were suspended between her disheveled locks as if they were diamonds. Pretty Lina, swimming in the water in an egg-yellow swimsuit that someone had discarded for having gone out of style and which was a little too big for her.

With Lina were her three friends: Clarice, Casimiro, and Damião. They were playing, turning leaves into small boats with crews that consisted of tiny men made with matches. Life, at that moment, was atrociously happy. A severe happiness that would later charge interest and monetary correction.

That moment in Clarice's life was called *before everything*. She could not have imagined, and, nonetheless, everything was so tenuous, fragile, like a loose tooth or the thread of a spider web.

The water in the river hit Clarice at her waist. Under her black swimsuit her breasts had grown and they were like small, fresh, ripe pears. It was summertime and she was turning thirteen that summer. Thirteen summers. She thought about that and said out loud: as a matter of fact, if I was born in the summer, then I'm turning thirteen years old but I have been alive for *fourteen* summers.

The other children didn't understand her mathematics, they stared at her for a moment and turned back to their play. Then they all clustered together on the river bank and gathered up a fistful of clay and Clarice made a sculpture. It was already past five and the sky was deepening into a dark cobalt blue when they left.

We can play again tomorrow, Clarice said.

She wore her skirt and blouse over her swimsuit and had on sandals. She arrived home fluttering like a butterfly that flutters over a forbidden quarry and sees everything but imagines nothing. Her father was sitting in the living room, in a mustard-colored recliner and her mother was in town, shopping. She had taken a maid along to help her. Maria Inês was off somewhere (maybe at the top of the forbidden quarry, covered in ticks and with a triumphant smile on her face?) playing with that cousin João Miguel whom Clarice did not like—and who didn't like Clarice. She entered the house through the kitchen because she was wet and didn't want to dirty the living room floor. Clarice, docile demure submissive well-mannered polite discreet adorable.

She chose some clean clothes. A white eyelet blouse lined in white cotton, yellow panties trimmed in white lace. A pair of light blue polyester shorts that were a little hot but Clarice adored them, above all because of the flowers embroidered close to the waist. And her leather-strapped sandals.

A butterfly was flying over the quarry.

That afternoon, he came. An adult, mature, a man.

A man who walked into her bedroom and sat her down on his lap and she wasn't afraid, at first, because that man was her father.

They both laughed. They talked a little. He caressed her hands.

He caressed her arms. Her shoulders, her breasts.

Clarice froze like a rabbit that has a premonition about its predator. The eagle flying low. She then tried to free herself but his arm was strong. And his lips on the base of her neck made her heart beat faster.

Her nausea remained caught at the entrance to her stomach until the still distant day that she would make the decision to abandon her husband and would bounce on the bus ride from Jabuticabais to Friburgo. She would vomit into a plastic bag and receive a look of disapproval from the passenger in front of her.

The man's hand on a very white breast. The nipple that he twisted as if winding a watch. A man's hand on Clarice's smooth stomach and his breath panting hatefully and his slacks where a mass appeared. The zipper that he unzipped with his right hand while the left hand looked for something between her thighs. His eyes closed. Her eyes frozen wide open.

Clarice, docile demure submissive well-mannered polite discreet adorable.

He would do that again. And again. And again. And in different ways. One day he actually lay on top of her and thrust his adult man's body into her young girl's body while she felt the taste of blood because she was biting her own lips so hard. His hands grasping her thighs so hard that afterwards bruises would appear there. His tongue moistening (blemishing) the inside of her ears and licking her color-drained lips and sweeping through her mouth so as not to leave any secret standing.

Again and again and again. Until Otacília decided to send her away in a taxi with two suitcases. Too late.

When Afonso Olímpio left her bedroom, Clarice didn't cry. She went to the bathroom. She didn't vomit. She took another bath. Something had shattered within her without making a sound.

She must have done *something* for her father to act like that. Not that all of that was a punishment, not by any means. But, maybe, just a response? Just as Otacília's cold eyes must also be a response? She would never find an explanation.

Otacília knew what was happening in her own house, in her own family, long before she finally took a stand. And no one said a single word. And Maria Inês ran away spilling her precious cypress seeds in the hall, the day she saw the two of them in the bedroom. The man and the girl. Her father. Her sister Clarice.

Docile demure submissive well-mannered polite discreet. Adorable.

June Festivities

Maria Inês's burning eyes were spawned the moment she saw her own father with Clarice, winding the nipple of her sister's breast and burying his face in her hair.

Maria Inês was carrying a treasure in her hands, and it fell to the ground and was broken to bits. She could never again believe in the value of a handful of cypress seeds. Her thoughts became those of a war strategist. Camouflaged, armed to the teeth, and prepared for anything. Maria Inês organized reality as best she could within the tight space of her nine years of age. She opened drawers. She closed drawers. She threw away old things and new things as well because, although they were new, they no longer fit her. Overnight: like magic. As if she had woken up and her feet had grown bigger and she had to get rid of all her shoes, even the prettiest, even her brand new imported ballet slippers.

She opened some doors and closed others and carefully locked that many others. She sealed windows with nails and pieces of wood, covered holes with duct tape. And she created masks for herself, as if she were playing at being an actress. Even her child's play, however, became serious. Grave child's play with deep frowns.

She saw Clarice leave for Rio de Janeiro in a taxi the morning they discovered Lina on the side of the road. And deep inside she improvised a semblance of a prayer for her sister.

Afonso Olímpio never went close to Maria Inês, he pretended to ignore her. But he was afraid of that younger daughter as if she were the devil itself. And in those days perhaps Maria Inês was indeed the devil. Deliberately—the best defense consisting in, since the beginning of time, attack.

Clarice went to Rio, she studied for a while. She came straight back to the altar of the small church in Jabuticabais. Then Otacília's illness grew worse and she died. It was precisely during the following year that that piercing look in Maria Inés's blazing eyes matured. It reached the exact point to be served and tasted, and it was of an excellent vintage.

The mass in honor of Otacília's memory on the first anniversary of her death had not yet been celebrated. It was the month of June, 1976. Throughout Brazil things were happening on the sly and at that very moment there were torturers engaged in the task of making political prisoners confess (to anything) or go mad. Or, of course, an easy but undesirable option: die. In the torture sessions there was usually a physician to evaluate how many beatings the prisoner could take, or how many electric shocks, or how many drownings.

"*Si ch'io vorrei morire*," Bernardo Águas would sing in a Monteverdi madrigal.

Afonso Olímpio had become a pitiful drunk. Sometimes Clarice would drop by to visit him, her father and enemy, but always in the company of her husband.

Maria Inês could not understand that. She herself wanted to forget him completely. Never see him again, never again have to look at those hands and link them to the blazing memory of the day she had caught a glimpse of them on the pale breast of a young girl.

At the same time, she knew that she would still have to face him one day. At least once, one last time.

Maybe Clarice also knew that and was just stalling for time with her visits. Ilton Xavier suffered through them and afterwards felt forced to comment: your poor father, so depressed after Dona Otacília's death.

That's what Ilton Xavier would say. And then he'd lie on top of the spread to read his Simenon.

For the June Festivities in honor of St. John, Clarice made the traditional sweets: white and black coconut *cocadas* and *pé-de-moleque* peanut pralines and bowls of hominy-coconut *canjica* mush.

Maria Inês came from Rio de Janeiro because the June festivities were the only ones she truly loved. The straw hats with fake braids and the freckles painted on cheeks with eyeliner. Mouths with blackened teeth to suggest missing teeth, other mouths with real missing teeth that ironically tried to hide behind closed-mouth smiles. Whoever could afford a costume wore one: pants with patches and plaid shirts and bandanas tied around their necks and high-topped boots. Colorful dresses with ruffles to the knees and high white socks. Those who could not afford costumes ended up, at any rate, blending in, in pants with patches that covered real holes and boots that were work shoes and party shoes too and only used when necessary. With flowery calico dresses that were saved for Sunday Mass (stored in drawers with bars of soap) and wool jackets on top, due to the cold.

There were also the games: the apple dance, musical chairs, fishing for prizes, written love messages (that didn't work very well because the majority of the people there couldn't read or write). And the good feeling showered down by the colorful banners strung up on long cord strips blessing it all. Corn-on-the-cob, *curau* corn and cinnamon pudding, sweet *paçoca* peanut squares. The huge bonfire. Everyone gathered around it and forgot about the night's cold and the children would later dare each other to jump over it, and hear the older ones: whoever plays with fire wets the bed.

That night, Maria Inês took her sister by the arm and square-danced with her, saying since you're not wearing a costume, Clarice, you can be the man.

Afonso Olímpio did not go to the party, and everyone understood that his period of mourning was not over. They felt sorry for him, the widower Afonso Olímpio at home alone.

People in general felt sorry for Afonso Olímpio and even tolerated his vice of alcohol, because he had the face and the demeanor of a victim. And they said that daughter who lives in Rio de Janeiro should come keep him company. Oh, but that's how children are, we raise them, give them all our love and afterwards, nothing. Ungrateful brats.

The ungrateful daughter jumped over the bonfire with the children and felt her face burn in the cold of the night. She held up the hem of her skirt, revealing her knee-high white socks. In her patent leather shoes, her feet soared high against the dark starless sky and her braids danced in the air, and she held the straw hat firmly to her head with her left hand.

That night Maria Inês was very happy. And Clarice, in everyday clothes, watched her, and the orange glow of the bonfire reflected in her face and her eyes. It was possible to make out two small twin bonfires dancing in Clarice's eyes.

When Ilton Xavier's parents' yard finally settled down to sleep, and the last embers of the bonfire extinguished, it was past three. The servants picked up paper plates and cups strewn about here and there. Ilton Xavier came up and, just to be safe, kicked the ground with his feet and covered the top of the dead bonfire with dirt, to make sure it was all the way out. Then he walked over to Clarice.

Are you coming?

In a little while.

She glanced at her sister and he understood that they wanted some time alone and, even though it was very late and his thermometer was registering forty degrees, he did not object.

Maria Inês was sitting off, on a low stone wall, her dusty patent leather shoes lightly grazing the ground. Clarice went over to her and as she walked she looked back and saw the shape of the last servant disappear into the dark, white scarf on her hair, dressed all in white, looking more like a phantom. There were owls hooting nearby and other nocturnal birds. A big willow tree poured its weeping branches onto the ground, and the sound of nearby running water could be heard.

Clarice put her arm around Maria Inês's waist but they didn't look at each other. They didn't speak, they just sat there motionless, close to one another, their lips purple from the cold and their cheeks chaffed from the cold, in the starless night. Looking at the hill that hid their childhood home, Otacília and Afonso Olímpio's house. Where things happened on the sly. Where he, the father, was sleepless and alone and drunk, looking in the direction of the hill that blocked the view of his daughters who called to him with their thoughts, like two witches.

Maria Inês woke up late with a headache, but smiled to see she hadn't wet the bed. She was staying in the guest room, which was next to the room occupied by her sister and Ilton Xavier.

She looked at her own reflection in the oval mirror of the dressing table. She picked up a brush and with the same hand got a bottle of water and half filled a glass and fumbled in her toiletry kit in search of an aspirin. Then she stopped in front of the mirror and slowly combed her hair. She put a robe on top of her flannel pajamas and went to the Breakfast Room where breakfast would be on the table. Waiting for her.

Clarice's father-in-law was sitting at the head of the table, one hundred percent comfortable in his role as the Great Patriarch, with his combed moustache and his gleaming riding boots. He had put the leather crop he used on his horse right there on the table, like people do with their car keys.

You woke up late, he said. I've already been to the corral and then to Jabuticabais to buy kerosene and back and now I'm having my second breakfast.

Last night we went to bed very late. And I woke up with a headache.

Would you like an aspirin?

I already took one, thank you.

Coffee's good for headaches. Have some.

They talked about banalities. Maria Inês noticed that his lips barely moved beneath his full gray moustache. When he heard the clock strike ten, he stood up, agile, athletic, saying now you'll have to excuse me. I have several things to do before lunch.

Later, Maria Inês finally decided to look for Clarice who was mysteriously absent that morning. She found her sister's mother-in-law in the kitchen with the maids and asked, by any chance, have you seen Clarice this morning?

Yes, I have. She said she was going to take a walk. She took off down the road. I think she went in the direction of your father's house.

Did she go with Ilton Xavier?

He's gone to the cooperative. Clarice went out alone.

Maria Inês thanked her and left the kitchen. She was calm as she crossed the plantation house from one end to the other, hearing her shoes tap a hollow sound on the wooden floor. She reached the front door that was open and went down the five steps that fed into the yard, crossed the central alley, and followed the small path that led to the main road. There were clouds in the sky, but there was no threat of rain. And she turned left, in the direction that would lead her to her father's front door. She didn't exactly intend to go there, however. She had a vague idea where to find Clarice.

She skirted Afonso Olímpio's house taking care not to be seen. And she trudged up the hill, crossing the pasture where meditative cows ruminated. She was going to be covered in ticks, but it wouldn't be the first time. Then she went through the woods along a faint trail that she herself had passed by numerous times. She saw the same trees and that trunk covered in thorns that she had inadvertently grabbed one day, with her inexperienced hands. Now she knew all the traps and she had a sixth sense for surprises. Countless roots crossed the path, but Maria Inês no longer tripped over them.

When she reached the quarry, she was sweating. She took off her sweater and tied it in a knot around her waist and squinted because the gray morning brightness bothered her eyes.

Silhouetted against the sky, Clarice's motionless figure looked like a wild animal. Maria Inês almost believed that if she made any brusque movements she would frighten her and scare her away.

Clarice saw her sister arriving, but she didn't look surprised.

I slept very badly last night, she said. I woke up early. You were still in your room, I waited for you for a while but then I decided to come here. I knew you would manage to find me.

Clarice's voice echoed among the rocks and softly slid down to Maria Inês, who said years and years ago João Miguel and I planted some coins up here. To see if a money tree would grow.

She drew a thin line in the dirt between two rocks with her foot.

And did it? Clarice asked.

Not yet. They must have been bad seeds, Maria Inês said and smiled.

She came closer. She climbed up the rocks with the intimacy of someone who knew the terrain well, with the ease of a beloved daughter in her mother's lap. Next to Clarice, a multicolored butterfly was poised and opened and closed its wings in slow movements, as if it were stretching itself. There below, the Ipês Farm. Clarice commented: they're plowing a pasture. They must have rented out part of the land.

Then they looked at each other, and Clarice asked the question she had put off for so many years, with words that almost sounded casual, you saw, didn't you? That day those cypress seeds you used to hoard appeared scattered all over the hall floor.

Maria Inês nodded.

I think our mother knew, said Clarice.

And didn't do anything about it.

She sent me to live in Rio.

Too late.

Maybe she couldn't before.

Maria Inês sighed and looked around. The wind was blowing softly up there and the perspiration began to dry on her face.

And now? she asked.

And now it's what you see. He drinks all the time, but a long time ago he decided to leave me alone. Besides, because today, I'm an adult.

But what he did.

Sometimes I just don't know, I don't know if I can bear it much longer. But, then again, I've managed to bear it all these years, haven't I.

Maria Inês could only imagine, which was not very much. There was a large spectrum of shared feelings, but also something that belonged only to her, to Maria Inês. And if it was all about secrets, the truth was there really weren't any, in fact. An impartial observer might classify them as mere formalities.

Perhaps it was, however, nothing more than a formality that led Afonso Olímpio to the quarry on that morning. That led his wobbly steps and his labored breath up the hill, through the pasture, through the woods.

He had seen Maria Inês approach and take the path that led to the pasture. He imagined where she was headed. And for the first time he decided to follow her, perhaps because he now needed to change the course of the story, even if he himself had been at the helm, so many years earlier. Because at night the silence of that living-dead house invaded his ears, his pores, his very thoughts. With a thousand sharpened claws, with a million gnawing teeth. The world he had erected for himself and was now only loneliness.

He was old. He looked years older than the last time Maria Inês had seen him, a year earlier. He appeared among the trees like a veiled threat, but he posed no threat, he had no more power for that. He was a dried-out branch, a dried-out man. Armed with a disjointed discourse with which he intended to conjugate words for the first time, words he was no longer able to comprehend.

His daughters saw him coming and didn't move. They followed him with their eyes. He stopped a few yards away, at the foot of the quarry. Quiet, because the words didn't obey when he tried to tap them from his memory. His life had been a good life. At times Afonso Olímpio felt guilty, but at times he deposited the same guilt outside himself: on Clarice. On Otacília, who had remained silent. On Maria Inês, who had been a witness.

Maria Inês felt the skin on the nape of her neck bristle, as if she were a cat, and asked with a loud voice so that he could hear from where he was: what's going on? What are you doing up here?

Don't talk to him like that, Clarice fussed.

In front of Maria Inês and Clarice, standing among those rocks like an apparition, his thin hair fluttering, Afonso Olímpio saw the face of the things that he could have done, but had not. And also the darkness of the things he should not have done, but had nonetheless done. A man missing the best part of himself, the part that would now have been able to hold him erect. Do you believe in hell, Father? Maria Inês asked.

Later, Clarice did what she was accustomed to doing and didn't cry. She didn't get sick. She didn't go crazy. She stayed awake all night at her father's wake, and her thoughts were like abstract paintings. Those present interpreted the blank look in her eyes to be grief, but it wasn't.

Crime and punishment, she thought. But that wasn't worth anything. Because lives and the feelings that guide lives are not mathematical.

What things were reserved for her? For Maria Inês? For her parents? What was the name of the hell that watched over the earth, in the light of man's reason? The bodies of young girls violated by their own fathers? The tortured bodies of political prisoners? The small bodies, full of worms and botflies and chigoe fleas, of the children who worked in the fields from sunrise to sunset?

For that reason, Clarice didn't cry, she didn't go crazy. She endured and continued to endure. Until one day, naturally, she cracked. With a hollow sound, just like the one her steps made on the floors of the old plantation house that belonged to Ilton Xavier's parents.

Maria Inês's resolute voice sounded like a splinter at the top of the quarry. Afonso Olímpio was mute. She repeated the question: do you believe in hell? You can answer. Up here there's only the two of us to hear your confession. Is that what you came up here to do? Confess?

She had begun. That was her black mass, which she had not planned but had awaited for so long. She unloosed the cords that had been strung tight inside of her since the moment her childhood had been violently snatched from her by a vision that could have, under other circumstances, been beautiful. Countless times she had dreamed that it had not been Clarice in his arms that afternoon, but Otacília. A happy Otacília. Or any other man with her sister. Another man: not her own father.

Why don't you just go away and get drunk and leave us alone?

Afonso Olímpio wanted to say everything that he had never felt like saying, but his efforts were useless. He took one step, two. Next to Clarice, the multicolored butterfly opened its wings and hurled itself into the abyss. It could fly. And see the recently plowed field at the Ipês Farm, the river below like a small golden thread.

The father's face was blank. He was devoid of the meaning of that name: father.

Earlier, when he had been in power, he had steered the story onto a course that gave him two enemies instead of two daughters.

The encounter was not, however, a classic case of guilt-regret-atonement. Nothing had names and nothing was defined. Because, in truth, nothing had changed and nothing would change and things had merely switched colors like the leaves on a tree with the succession of the seasons.

Afonso Olímpio began to climb up the quarry. He had been drinking that morning, and earlier, throughout the night. He was thin and had deep, purplish circles under his eyes.

Clarice went forward. Docile demure submissive well-mannered. Almost as if on impulse, a conditioned reflex. Maria Inês knew that she was going to try and help him. Obey, one more time.

Leave him be, Maria Inês said.

But Maria Inês, he's . . .

Let him be.

There was something at work in Afonso Olímpio. His body was covered in a cold, sticky sweat. Maria Inês held her sister by her hand. He continued to climb, hanging on to the larger rocks with his hands, out of breath. What the hell does he want, Maria Inês thought, and could not find any answer at all. What the hell did he want.

And then he reached the top and looked at his two daughters and held out his hand. Not that. Maria Inês grabbed Clarice by the waist and gently moved her away. And then Maria Inês went up to him and said I should have taken her far away from the beginning, but I was still very small. Now I'm all grown up, Father.

She surprised herself to hear herself saying that word, father. Then, very gently, she pushed. A minimum sound, almost inaudible, echoed in Clarice's mind, and she turned her face up to the sky and saw the image of the multicolored butterfly, soaring. That vision remained stuck in her dry eyes as her father's body fluids had earlier stuck to her thighs to the point that she had to use a washcloth to scrub them off.

Afterwards, Maria Inês softly led her among the rocks. The silence buzzed in Clarice's ears, but she did not look back. She did not even feel her father's pain, as he fell from the heights, his body, frightening the birds, the insects, the ghosts. On the other side, where there was nothing. Where, in the main house of the Ipês Farm, ghosts wandered, round snails very slowly scratched the sleeping walls and plants grew on the roof. She just followed, in spite of herself, as if she were a shadow of her own body.

It all happened so fast, Maria Inês's hand on his chest, pushing. And perhaps his eyes saying it's fine like this. It was not exactly pity that Clarice felt, but a slight detachment, as if she were watching a film. And she let Maria Inês lead her down, down the hill, through the woods and the field where cattle ruminated and small ticks waited.

The Open Door

Things always appear less devastating when seen up close. They lose their sacredness, they become common everyday things. They reduce that distance between themselves and the idea of themselves.

Tomás didn't know where that open door would lead him, but he had an immovable faith in free will—an acquired skill, an exercised muscle. As such he was not frightened. He knew his own steps and forged his own paths the same way a music arranger chooses chords for a particular melody and instruments to give sound to those chords and musicians to play those instruments.

So he walked up to the house and found the two sisters on the front porch, their features softened by the twilight, which imparted a dream-like texture to everything.

Maria Inês said, as she stood up to greet him, so we all end up getting together here.

A very improbable situation, he said, looking at her and inadvertently remembering some hippie fair jewelry she used to wear twenty years earlier.

Maybe not all that improbable, she said.

Now her neck was bare, serious. Tomás felt a closed fist in his chest. And then he felt it loosen its grip.

Clarice returned Tomás's greeting and remained quiet.

Maria Inês said my daughter went to take a quick nap. We woke up early today.

Clarice then stood up very slowly. I'm going inside to take care of some things.

Clarice went to find something to do. Drink a glass of water. Take a peek at the food that Fátima, so thoughtfully, had left prepared for their dinner. Wash her face the heat had made oily, wash her hands. Walk out the back door and take the path to the corral and visit some old sculptures that were kept there, in the back of a cabinet, like a museum. Then close the cabinet and leave them waiting there until another moment.

She tried to imagine what Tomás and Maria Inês might be saying to one another. If they were talking about trivialities, weather age work appearance trips or if they were silent, trapped in an intense awkwardness. If they were exchanging pleasantries like preambles—to what? If they were secretly considering going back twenty years in time (*time stands still, but creatures*) and take up their story on the last day they had seen and loved one another.

A bat flew close to Clarice, a swift stain against the darkening sky. Then another, and still another. Or was it the same one, triplicated? She raised her eyes and noticed that the stars were beginning to appear. She leaned against the corral gate and watched as the stars slowly multiplied.

When she went back to the house neither Maria Inês nor Tomás were there. Eduarda was alone in the living room, her hair wet from her recent bath and lavender perfume floating through the air.

I thought my mother was with you, Eduarda said.

No. She's with Tomás.

Eduarda nodded and said she came to the farm to see that man, besides you.

Yes, I think so.

Where did they go?

I don't know.

Are we going to have dinner now or wait for her?

Whatever you want.

So let's wait a little longer. Is that okay?

Sure.

Maria Inês only came back much later. It was past eleven. She didn't say a word, or, like a young girl, offer any excuses for arriving too late for dinner. She went to the kitchen to heat something up in a pan because there wasn't a microwave oven there.

Clarice went with her without asking any questions (Clarice would never ask any questions about that night) while Eduarda stayed in the living room with her guitar. Strumming chords and singing *Do you miss me, Miss Misery, like you say you do* in her weak voice.

The small path had been used so many times that Clarice could have easily followed it with her eyes blindfolded. From long before, since her childhood. Even after everything had changed that path remained the same. The dirt went through phases there: in the rainy season, it acquired ruts and small lakes where butterflies would later gather by the dozen. In the dry season, it hardened and flaked. It was almost always soiled with horse dung, at times with goat dung as well, but it was always the same path.

In the wee hours of the morning it was more beautiful. It was calmer and could pretend it was a piece of ground on the moon, with pebbles reflecting a milky, surreal light. To the side, in the pasture, behind the barbed wire fence, the cattle slept. Almost everything slept, and Clarice walked along that small path that led to the old farmhand's house. But she was not in a hurry.

Maria Inês and Eduarda had stayed at the house, closed up in their respective rooms, silent, sleeping or not. Clarice had sat with Maria Inês at the dining room table, and smiled to realize that it was good to have her home after all. The pendulum clock struck midnight, twelve gongs, and no yellow devils appeared and no Cinderellas had to flee in haste. And the clock struck one. And later still, when the house had gone to sleep, Clarice went out. Into the night, to look for and find an open door.

The lights in his house were on, the old farmhand's house. Clarice stopped at the threshold, on the rug made of cloth scraps, and said I knew that you wouldn't be asleep yet.

I doubt if I'll sleep, Tomás said.

I can imagine.

Come on in. We can make some tea. I have a can here that Cândido brought me from a trip. Would you like some?

I'd love some.

They went into the kitchen and Clarice filled the dented aluminum teapot with water and commented Maria Inês says people should only use stainless steel pans, or cast iron, or earthenware, because aluminum can cause dementia after a few years. It accumulates in the brain, or something. Did you know that?

No, Tomás said, but at any rate I only have aluminum pots and pans.

He got down the beige can of Earl Grey tea. Without his glasses he could no longer read the tiny letters that said *By appointment to Her Majesty Queen Elizabeth II. Tea and coffee merchants R. Twin-*

ing & Co. Ltd. London. They put the water on to boil. Tomás didn't own any special gadgets for making tea, so they put two spoons of the Earl Grey into the teapot and then they poured it through a strainer.

English tea, by chance. They remained silent for a while, seated on the floor of the porch. Even at that hour it was hot. Then Tomás answered the question that Clarice had not asked.

She was here, you know. But it wasn't exactly like I'd imagined it would be.

Clarice continued to stir her cup of tea with the spoon. And confessed: at first I didn't like the idea that she was coming.

I didn't either. But that was our mistake, because we held her responsible for too much.

And what about Eduarda?

I should have looked her up sooner, of course, but things are never that way, all neat and tight like a movie script.

And Tomás recognized that he had truly been afraid, and why. Like an alcoholic who's been on the wagon for years and suddenly, at a ritzy party, finds himself face to face with a shot of whiskey. Afraid of himself and of his passion. However, if that passion was still a part of him, of his life, the object of his passion could only exist in the past. In fact he was now abandoning Maria Inês one more time, decades after he had been abandoned by her.

Clarice's face reflected the light coming from the living room, a face lit up like a beacon in the middle of the night. And he asked do you remember how many years I've lived here?

No, she answered.

Neither do I. I can't remember.

Tomás placed his hand softly on Clarice's shoulder, on her dark blue dress with light blue flowers. She didn't smile. Somewhere close by an owl hooted. Tomás waited and observed that small infinity as her arm moved to touch his arm, his back. Not as thin as in the past, when he was twenty years old. Then she came closer and rested her forehead on his face.

It would never be possible to forget. Clarice knew that. There was also no such thing as an innocuous memory, a cauterized wound, a beast without claws and teeth, merely existing. The reconciliation of the past with everything it carried. A city existed in Clarice's memory, a city destroyed by war or by an earthquake, but now, there were new buildings and the debris had been removed and the dead had been buried.

Her lips and Tomás's lips did not know exactly where to begin and so they began on each other, lips, mouths, and the moths and other insects flew in imperfect circles around the bare light bulb, in the living room.

Clarice holds his head with her two hands, as if it were a sculpture, and her fingers softly tug on his graying hair. Very softly. And helps his lips find the path to her chin, to the base of her neck, to the seam of her dress. Now Tomás holds (very gently) her breasts with his two hands, as if they were a sculpture. Now she unbuttons his shirt and uncovers his thin chest, now she is going to kiss him there, in the exact spot where she can feel with her lips his beating heart. Fast. Faster. And now he unbuttons her dress and counts the buttons, one, two, three, four, five, and then his hands on her back find the hooks of her bra. Now she looks at the immense sky and the mountains, and the static night air finds the bared skin of her chest and he is going to place his lips there, where she was not waiting for him, where she was not expecting him.

Now her hand finds the surface of his pants, his thighs, his hips. And she is now caressing his graying hair again and he discovers the valley of her stomach. Now she makes him stand up and unzips his jeans.

Now he lifts her and sits her on the porch bench, on the edge. It is not, however, about a pedestal, but about a mere woman. He buries his face in her neck, in her hair, and he sees her bare left earlobe, no earring glimmering there.

Nothing is easy. By any means. However, if it is true that time stands still (and only creatures pass by), everything that matters is germinated in the present moment. Not with the intention to flourish or bear fruits, but solely to germinate. To be a seed. To say *now*—which, thus, simply means another way of saying: always.

The Soul of the World

It's wintertime in Europe, in Italy. Maybe João Miguel will decide to stop by Venice to see a handsome Paolo again, now not so young, perhaps even more handsome. But no: Maria Inês doesn't know, she has no way of knowing if the ex-young Paolo is now living in Rome and working at a serious job. Maybe he's a lawyer and lives in a beautiful apartment and has a family.

Maria Inês slept little during the night and had time to think about the Italian winter, and remember once more the Café Florian, and forget it once more. To remember the time when she was a Whistler painting, when she lived with her Great-Aunt Berenice. And remember the circumspect time of her great-aunt's death: natural causes. A year after Venice and the Florian Café and the still-young, handsome Paolo.

She had time to remember the clinic where Clarice finally admitted herself, with an inner patio populated by tacky sculptures: the kind manufactured in series and sold on the edges of highways. In one corner stood Snow White and the Seven Dwarfs and, close by, an uncomfortably stiff heron. Farther away, a giant frog, an eyesore. There were, however, lovely plants. The climate in the mountains is usually generous to plants. There were even hydrangeas in undulating flowerbeds that the inmates themselves cared for. One afternoon, when Maria Inês had gone to the clinic to visit her, Clarice was sitting on the far end of a recently painted white wooden bench. It was cold and she was wrapped in a wool blanket. She was drinking tea—a lemon tea brewed by the nurse and served in a plastic cup like the ones used at children's parties. Clarice raised her face and looked in the direction of the mountains and said hi to her sister and asked about her niece and if she would go visit her at the farm when she left the clinic.

It is wintertime in Italy and summertime on the farm where Maria Inês lies on the bed of the guest room and sees, through the blue-shuttered window, the morning coming to life little by little. *Fiat lux.*

It is still very early when she finally gets out of bed and opens the window and does what she always used to do as a child: to go outside, skipping the bureaucratic passage through a ton of doors and rooms. She finds something to step up on, takes it over to the window, and hoists herself up with her two hands. Perched on the window sill, she swings her legs around and leaps down to the narrow cement sidewalk, now cracked in several places, that borders the exterior of the house.

During the night Maria Inês was able to take a vague inventory of herself as she listened to the pendulum clock in the living room strike the hours. She could almost be certain she would not dream about Bernardo Águas anymore—her university classmate who, after their course of study ended, abandoned a medical career in favor of another, an international one, as a singer (*Si ch'io vorrei morire*), who once called to catch up on things and ended up becoming her lover—after the emerald rings, after Venice. Long after Tomás. The one who identified her as a statistic—a colored pin on a map of the world. Her false haven. Her biggest cliché.

Maria Inês now walks barefoot on the grass. There is a gentle presence there: the soul of the world. *Anima mundi*. She walks over to the empty cement pool, where ferns grow out of the cracked bottom. In the old days she used to swim there. When she was still a child and it would take her six or seven strokes to cross the span of the pool. It was there she had learned to open her eyes underwater and dive without having to hold her nose with her thumb and index finger and to do somersaults underwater—forwards and, more difficult, backwards. She looks at the bottom of the pool and at the fern leaves that unroll like viable futures. Like unviable futures, as well.

Nonetheless, in the end, the journey holds no surprises for her, simply because the surprises unroll within the journey, like the fern leaves. How can she be relevant for her sister and her old lover who walk in the light of day on that farm from her past? Are they like ghosts unaware of their condition?

No matter if a thousand and one fantasies are sculpted. After it is all said and done, life is like mathematics—with operations that escape the norm and numbers that produce improbable results, where dividends and divisors at times constitute a subtraction or a multiplication. Mathematics: Achilles and the tortoise. Then she remembers a second cousin on the edge of a honey-colored lake where gladiator frogs croak everywhere and a group of ducks gathers at the margin. There are dragonflies buzzing over the surface of the water, and the singing of nocturnal birds blends in with the singing of tardy diurnal birds that are probably moving into the night shift, working overtime.

Maria Inês knows that Clarice was absent a good part of the night. It's not hard to guess where she was, and in whose company. However, she imagines that there are no predictions to be made.

For herself, Maria Inês, there are none either. In truth, there is no need to do the accounting for years past or years to come. And nothing new. Nothing new. And yet, everything is new. *Fiat lux*.

She takes the path that circles the pool and goes by some chayote vines. Clarice has been planting chayote. And cherry tomatoes, which are eaten whole and explode festively with each bite. She then sees some eucalyptus trees that sprouted two or three decades earlier. Bromeliads multiply. Small plants grow and adult plants die. At the top of a bare hill there is a blackened trunk stump where once grew an enormous ipê.

Maria Inês continues to follow the narrow trail that will lead into the main road. She has no specific destination in mind. She is simply walking, one foot, then the other. Yes, she will go back home later, for breakfast and all the rest. At this moment, however, she does not look back, and as she walks she can feel the rising sun on her back.

The morning floats up from the road in dust. Everything is quiet, or almost quiet, while a man with eyes wide open pretends to watch the road. In fact, Tomás has already made his decision. But he waits, because it is still early and he's familiar with that habit so precious to young people of waking up at noon. He remembers his youth. When he was twenty years old and his mornings began at noon.

He waits. He lights a cigarette, smokes. He greets Jorgina with a nod when she arrives for work and listens to the guinea fowl repeat their litany and observes the dog scratch itself with its hind paw. Then he leisurely takes the road and goes to meet his daughter Eduarda.

I'll bet we've already swallowed a bunch of guava worms, Maria Inês said and stared provocatively at her sister. Can you imagine, Clarice? A piece of a worm, a head, a tail, that squishy white thing. A *worm*!

Stop it, Maria Inês! For Pete's sake!

Maria Inês stopped talking and took another bite of her guava and stared into the distance. At a man on horseback passing by on the road in his straw hat. Their mother was at home sewing. Their father had gone into town to buy some medicine. They were simply that, then: mother, father. Potential friends.

What happened to your leg? Clarice asked, pointing to a scratch on Maria Inês's thin thigh.

I hurt it yesterday. I fell off the swing.

You swing too high.

I like to.

But you can fall and hurt yourself.

That's okay. I don't care.

Then the two girls became silent and observed the world from the top of the guava tree. Leisurely, without fear. They were not yet afraid, there were no monsters yet, breathing in the shadows of their house: only the future—that sparkled with expectations just as their eyes sparkled at that moment.

Clarice thought she would make a sculpture to give to Maria Inês for Christmas. And Maria Inês wondered if a handful of cypress seeds would be a good present for her sister, or if she was too grown up for those things—Clarice was already eleven years old, after all. Then something somber passed through her heart and she discreetly moved closer to her sister and put her arm around her waist. The shadow moved on and Maria Inês smiled again and said, on impulse: I love you.

They looked at the mountains and tried to guess what might lie beyond them. They looked into the future and tried to guess what might lie there, waiting for them. Like worms inside guavas or like unopened Christmas presents. Tickets to the opera or maybe love letters? High heels and lipstick, long fingernails?

Clarice placed her arm around Maria Inês's shoulder and imagined what it would be like when they would meet, as adults. In Rio de Janeiro. Or in Paris. A famous ballerina and a famous sculptor. With photographs of their husbands and children in their purses, with beautiful clothes and fragrant perfume. Filled with affection, she imagined that one day they would remember the day that they were eating guavas and Maria Inês said I'll bet we've already swallowed a bunch of guava worms.

Clarice was happy. It was radiant, the future she saw ahead. She had no doubts about it. She smiled at Maria Inês and said let's go, Lina promised to come over to play after lunch. Let's go.

And the two girls descended from the guava tree in one leap and ran home.